# WATCH HOLLOW

## THE ALCHEMIST'S SHADOW

# GREGORY FUNARO

# WATCH HOLLOW

## THE ALCHEMIST'S SHADOW

**HARPER**
*An Imprint of HarperCollinsPublishers*

Library of Congress Control Number: 2019946111

ISBN 978-0-06-264348-3

Typography by Jessie Gang

20 21 22 23 24   PC/LSCH   10 9 8 7 6 5 4 3 2 1

First Edition

*For David, for MiNa;*

*and, as always, for my daughter.*

"Unhappy is he to whom the memories of childhood bring only fear and sadness."

—H. P. Lovecraft

# PROLOGUE

"What took you so long?" the old man croaked, and Bedelia Graves stepped into the darkened study. Her employer was sitting in his wheelchair just outside a shaft of light from the hallway—his withered frame a lump of shadow in the gloom.

"My apologies, sir," said Ms. Graves. "I didn't mean to keep you waiting, but Algernon had some trouble falling asleep."

"Excited about the move to the States?"

"No doubt, sir," said Ms. Graves, dropping her eyes. She was lying. Algernon had had a nightmare—or at least, that was what Ms. Graves assumed. The boy hadn't spoken in nearly two years, so it was often hard to tell. Nevertheless, of one thing she was certain: Algernon *hated* the idea of moving to the States.

But one did not complain to a man like Oscar Snockett.

"Perhaps it's that doll of his—that *Kenny*," he said. "Never mind the boy's absurd attachment to such a thing, the smell of it is enough to wake the dead."

Ms. Graves could not see the old man's face in the darkness, but she could tell by the tone of his voice that he was smiling. Ms. Graves nodded and smiled back. True, the fact that a twelve-year-old boy should be attached to "such a thing" *was* a bit absurd—not to mention, Kenny did smell like sour milk. His clothes were tattered, his hair was tangled, and the tip of his nose was missing. But without Kenny, Ms. Graves thought, Algernon might never sleep again.

"And what of—the other one?" asked Mr. Snockett. "That snarky girl?"

"Agatha, sir," Ms. Graves said gently. "And she went out like a light."

Mr. Snockett heaved a wheezing sigh. "The way a child should be," he said. "Quiet, respectful, and obedient. Smelly dolls aside, I'll grant you've done well by them this past year."

Ms. Graves pressed her lips together tightly. She'd been governess to the Kojima twins for nearly *two* years—but one did not correct a man like Oscar Snockett.

"And what about you, Ms. Graves?" the old man said, his wheelchair squeaking. "Are you excited to leave your native England and take up at Blackford House? I'm certainly paying you quite handsomely."

Mr. Snockett was leaning forward now, closer to the light. His sagging, shriveled face looked like a skull in the shadows—his cheeks hollow, his eyes empty and black and yet piercing just the same. Ms. Graves swallowed hard. Even here, in the darkened study, she felt as if Oscar Snockett could see into her very soul. Mr. Snockett *was* paying her quite handsomely—not to mention, it had always been a secret dream of Bedelia Graves to move to the States. But in the end, that's not why she'd agreed to move.

"I'm content to look after the twins wherever you see fit, sir," said Ms. Graves. "We've grown quite fond of each other and . . . well, they need me, sir."

"Well, that's the *plan*, isn't it?" growled Mr. Snockett, and Ms. Graves's heart began to pound. One did not want to irritate a man like Oscar Snockett.

"I meant no disrespect, sir," said the governess. "I only wished to express my gratitude for being allowed to go on serving you and your family."

Mr. Snockett sneered. "My *family*," he said sarcastically. "A great-niece and great-nephew I'd never met until their parents up and died on them. Family indeed. If I wanted children about the place, I'd have had them decades ago."

Bedelia Graves remembered very little from decades ago. Granted, she was only thirty-two, but she felt much older. Perhaps it was because she'd spent so much time trying to forget her childhood that the memory of it seemed farther back than it really was. And what was there to remember anyway? Loneliness? A dingy flat in Leeds and the desperation to escape a father who treated her more like a servant than a daughter? Her mother had left them when Bedelia was ten, and the memories afterward were . . . well, not worth remembering.

All that changed, however, when Bedelia Graves came to work for The Agency at the age of nineteen. There had been other children, of course, but none like Agatha and Algernon Kojima. And in the two years since Oscar Snockett hired her to look after them in his dark and dreary mansion, Bedelia Graves had broken The Agency's cardinal rule: she'd grown to love them.

The governess cleared her throat and stood up straight. "You've been more than generous, sir. The children are forever in your debt. As am I."

"Are you now?"

A heavy silence hung about the room, and then Mr. Snockett's wheelchair squeaked and his face sank back into the shadows.

"In any event," he said, "Blackford House belongs to the twins. I never liked their father. I've made no secret of that. Prancing about with his silly puppets. But I've always had a soft spot for my niece, despite her going against my wishes and marrying that fool. Nasty business, sometimes. Family. But in the end, we Snocketts do take care of our own—no matter how *inconvenient*."

The old man had popped the final *t* of *inconvenient* so sharply that it sounded like a twig snapping. Ms. Graves flinched.

"I've personally seen to all the necessary arrangements," Mr. Snockett continued. "Immigration details, accounts, disbursement of your salary and whatnot. You and the twins shall be well provided for, but I do not wish to be troubled any further. Do you understand, Ms. Graves?"

"Very much so, sir."

Mr. Snockett dangled a large red jeweled pendant into the shaft of light and swung it back and forth like a hypnotist's charm. And for a moment, Ms. Graves *was* hypnotized. She just stood there, blinking, with her mouth ajar.

The pendant's single red jewel was glowing.

"For good luck on your journey," said Mr. Snockett.

"I—er—" the governess stammered, "I cannot accept such a gift, sir."

*"Take it!"* the old man snapped, and Ms. Graves obeyed. The red jewel was about the size of a fifty-pence coin, but it was no longer glowing. Quite the opposite; the jewel now looked black in Ms. Graves's hand. And it was ice cold.

The governess shivered.

"Wear it. Always," Mr. Snockett said with a magician's wave of his hand, and Ms. Graves felt dizzy. She shook her head, blinked, and in the next moment the dizziness lifted, and she clasped the pendant's chain around her neck. She didn't have a choice.

After all, one did not refuse a man like Oscar Snockett.

# ONE

# THE RIGHTFUL HEIRS

"Take it *back*!" Lucy shouted, and Billy Mahoney squealed in pain.

Lucy was on top of him now, pinning the boy on his stomach and twisting his arm behind his back. Billy tried to wriggle free, but Lucy wedged her thigh under his pudgy elbow and, shifting her weight, cranked his arm higher. Billy howled.

"Lucy, stop it!" cried her brother, Oliver, but Lucy just ignored him.

"You take back what you said, Billy Mahoney, or I'll break your arm!"

"Okay, okay, I take it back!"

"Take *what* back?"

"Frog-face! You're *not* a frog-face!"

Lucy let go of Billy and stood up—her fists ready just in case the bigmouth wanted to go a second round. But Billy, half-dazed and moaning, just rolled over and sat there rubbing his arm. The front of his Captain America T-shirt was filthy, and his chubby, freckled cheeks were beet red. Oliver tried to help him up, but Billy shook him off and rose unsteadily to his feet.

"You okay?" Oliver asked. Billy dragged his wrist under his nose. He was breathing hard, and Lucy could tell he was trying not to cry. For a long, tense moment there was only the buzz of insects and the soft babble of the river there in the woods, and then Billy narrowed his eyes at Lucy and said:

"Shoulda called you *psycho* instead."

Lucy set her teeth and lunged for him, but Oliver blocked her path and held her by the shoulders. His eyes were wide and pleading behind his glasses—Don't do this! Not here! those eyes said.

Lucy held his gaze for a moment, then sighed and uncurled her fists.

Oliver let go of her and pushed up his glasses.

"Let's just forget about it, okay?" he said, turning back to Billy—but Billy was already shuffling toward his bike. "Where you going?"

"I need to get back to the store," Billy said quietly. He grabbed his bike by the handlebars and began pushing it up the bank. Oliver swiveled his eyes between Lucy and Billy, and after an awkward silence, said:

"So, I guess I'll see you tomorrow, then?"

Billy shrugged, and a second later he was gone behind a clump of trees.

Lucy watched after him for a moment as Oliver picked up something off the ground. A crumpled bag of Skittles. Billy must've dropped it when she tackled him, Lucy figured, and a pang of guilt seized her heart. Billy was twelve, a year older than Lucy, but short for his age, like her. And he clearly knew nothing about fighting—which hardly made things fair. Lucy was an *expert* on fighting—not to mention she had really liked Billy up until he made that crack about her being a frog-face.

What happened? One minute the three of them were laughing and searching for turtles, and then the next . . .

"You shouldn't have done that," Oliver said, brushing some dirt off the Skittles. "Billy was just talking trash like you were."

Lucy opened her mouth and snapped it shut again. She *had* been talking trash. Something about seeing Billy's plumber's crack when he bent over—which was true, and not nearly as bad as calling someone a frog-face. But still, Lucy could hardly consider herself an innocent bystander.

"Anyway, don't do that again," Oliver said. "Billy's my friend."

Lucy frowned. At least Oliver *had* a friend here in Watch Hollow—which was one more than Lucy had. Billy's father owned the hardware store in town, and over the past two months, Oliver and Pop had gotten chummy with them. Billy's father even made Pop a member of the Rotary Club. Lucy wasn't quite sure what a Rotary Club was—only that her father thought it was a big deal and they didn't let kids in.

Lucy's eyes drifted back to the river. Oliver was right. Billy was just talking trash—and certainly no worse trash than idiots like Betty Bigsby used to talk back home in Massachusetts. But Lucy's home now was here in Watch Hollow, Rhode Island. And for some reason, Billy talking trash was just one more thing about this place that made her feel . . . well . . . *mixed-up* was the only word Lucy could think of at the time.

Lucy's stomach knotted. A thought had caught her by surprise, and yet Lucy understood on some level that it had been swimming around in her head for a while—just beneath the surface, like the turtles she sometimes caught in the shallow river. School would be starting next week. What if the kids here in Watch Hollow didn't like her? What if they called her a frog-face, too?

All this flashed through Lucy's mind in an instant, but when she met her brother's eyes again, he looked away and dragged his wrist across his brow.

Oliver didn't seem mixed-up these days. Just the opposite. Two months ago, his forehead and chin had been covered in pimples, but now his skin was clear and tan. The countless hours they'd spent outside had done wonders for his complexion. And not just that, Oliver's arms looked almost muscular now. He didn't spend nearly as much time cooped up inside with his comic books as before. In fact, Lucy couldn't remember a time when she'd seen her brother so happy—that is, until she screwed things up.

Lucy nervously fingered the single braid of her long black hair. Her heart felt twenty pounds too heavy for her chest. "I'm sorry," she said, and Oliver shoved the bag of Skittles into his pocket.

"Let's just forget about it."

But once they were back across the river, Lucy could tell that Oliver *hadn't* forgotten about it. He didn't say a word, didn't even look at her as they wound their way up the long dirt driveway toward Blackford House. There were no woods on this side of the river, only clusters of flowering trees and vast, gently sloping lawns—which was why, Lucy thought, out here in the sunlight, Oliver's anger seemed all the more real.

A lump rose in Lucy's throat and she bit her lip. If only she understood *why* things felt so mixed-up lately. Then again, there were a lot of things about Watch Hollow that Lucy didn't understand. And not understanding things in Watch Hollow always led to trouble. Look what happened to Mortimer Quigley. *He* thought he understood the way things worked around here, and accidentally brought back from the dead an evil alchemist named Edgar Blackford. As a result, the enormous clock in Blackford House stopped ticking. Mr. Quigley hired Lucy's father to fix it, but it was really Edgar Blackford, that vicious tree monster, who'd been pulling the strings. The Garr, the clock animals had called him.

The clock animals.

The lump rose higher in Lucy's throat. When she first arrived at Watch Hollow, the clock animals had been able to come alive. But now that the Garr was dead and the clock was fixed, they had to remain in its face as wooden statues. There were thirteen of them in all—one for each number and a cuckoo bird named Tempus Crow—but Lucy missed Torsten the dog, Fennish the one-eyed rat, and Meridian the cat most of all. They were the best friends she'd ever had; and yet, without them to power the clock, the magic in Blackford House wouldn't work.

Maybe that was it, Lucy said to herself as she looked around. Even though Watch Hollow was back to normal, things felt . . . well, *too normal*. Watch Hollow felt like any other stupid town. If only Torsten were alive again, Lucy thought. The little dog always knew how to make her smile.

At that moment, Lucy heard a car coming up the driveway—a silver BMW, she discovered once it was almost upon her. The children moved out of the way, and the car barreled past, kicking up so much dust that Lucy couldn't see who was inside.

Lucy and Oliver hurried after it, and by the time they

reached the house, they found the car parked beside their father's ancient pickup. Between the two vehicles stood a smartly dressed woman and two children with longish bobs of jet-black hair—a girl and a boy, Lucy realized as she drew closer. The girl wore a uniform like the private school snots wore back home, while the boy was dressed in shorts, a cardigan vest, and a bow tie. His long bangs were like a curtain over his eyes, and his argyle socks stretched up to his knees. They were the strangest-looking kids Lucy had ever seen. And even stranger, the boy was carrying a creepy samurai doll that was half as big as he was.

"Who are you?" the woman asked, her eyes flitting between Lucy and the truck. The woman's hair, done up tightly in a bun, was a deep red, but not quite as red as the large ruby pendant that hung about her neck. The jewel sparkled in the sunlight. Lucy felt hypnotized by it, and just blinked back at the woman blankly.

"There's no need to be afraid, young lady," the woman said gently. "We're just as surprised to see you as you are to see us."

The woman sounded British. Just like Mr. Quigley, Lucy thought, and the back of her neck prickled with dread. Lucy gulped and looked to Oliver for help.

"Er—my name's Oliver Tinker," he said. "And this is my sister, Lucy. We live here. With our father, I mean."

*"Here?"* the woman asked. "In Blackford House?"

"Uh-huh," Lucy said. "We're—you know—the care-takers."

"The *caretakers*?" the woman said, confused. Lucy nodded, and the woman eyed her skeptically down her long thin nose. "All right, then," she said, stiffening her spine. "Let's get to the bottom of this. Where is your father now?"

"Right here," he called from the porch. His sweatshirt was covered with grease and his curly red hair was all sweaty. Even though the clock was ticking perfectly now, for the past two months, Lucy's father had been working day and night on a fail-safe in case things ever went haywire again. No one wanted a repeat of what happened last time.

Mr. Tinker beamed as he bounded down from the porch; but as he drew closer, Lucy noticed her father's smile falter and his cheeks turn red. He chuckled nervously and, wiping the sweat from his brow, left a smear of grease there.

Lucy swiveled her eyes back to the woman, whose mouth was now turned up ever so slightly in a smile.

"I—er—Charles Tinker," he said, extending his hand. The woman eyed it coolly—the hand was too filthy to shake—and Lucy's father immediately pulled back and wiped it on his jeans.

"My name is Bedelia Graves," the woman said. "The Kojimas and I have come all the way from England to live

17

at Blackford House. The children are its legal heirs."

Lucy's heart seized, and she traded an anxious glance with Oliver. The way she understood things, there *were no heirs* to Blackford House—which was why the deed had been handed over to Pop. Lucy had seen it herself, right there in black and white. *Charles Tinker* was now the owner of Blackford House—not to mention, they'd already moved all their stuff from the city. And what they hadn't moved, they'd sold. The clock shop was totally empty now and had a For Rent sign in the window!

"I'm sorry," said Mr. Tinker, wringing the rag nervously in his hands, "but I don't understand. The legal heirs?"

"My employer is a gentleman by the name of Oscar Snockett," said Ms. Graves. "He is great-uncle to the twins and became their guardian upon the death of their parents. Mr. Snockett, however, is an old bachelor with no interest in children, and thus sent them to live here. Blackford House belongs to the Kojimas on their mother's side. Distant relations of the original owners, yes, but legitimate nonetheless."

"Allow me, Ms. Graves," said the girl, stepping forward. "My name is Agatha Kojima. I'm twelve years old, and despite the awkwardness of the situation, I am very pleased to make your acquaintance." Agatha gazed up at the house. "That said, rest assured that my brother and I are no more pleased about our arrival than you are. I have done quite a bit of research on Watch Hollow with the hopes it might induce in me a desire to live here. I regret to inform you that it has not." Agatha reached into her pocket and pulled out a handful of jelly beans. "Jelly bean, anyone?"

Lucy shook her head, and Agatha popped a jelly bean into her mouth. Ms. Graves put her arm around the boy.

"And this here is Algernon."

The boy gestured a quick hello, and then just stood there looking at Lucy with his nose raised slightly. Or at least, Lucy *thought* he was looking at her. It was hard to tell because Algernon's eyes were buried beneath his bangs. As for his samurai doll, its hair was a tangled mess, its silken robes were ragged and dirty, and its nose was broken off. The mouth was carved so that Lucy wasn't sure if the doll was smiling or clenching its teeth; and worst of all, the samurai's eyes were wide and bulging like a bug's—and they were staring straight at her.

"Well—er—nice to meet you both," said Mr. Tinker. "And who's your doll here, Algernon?"

Algernon made some quick gestures, and then Agatha stayed his hand.

"I don't think they know sign language, Algy," she said.

"Algernon doesn't speak," said Ms. Graves. "The doctors aren't quite sure what's wrong—only that it's the result of an injury he sustained during the accident."

"Accident?" asked Mr. Tinker.

"I'm afraid the twins lost their parents in a car accident. And in the two years since, we've learned to communicate with Algernon via sign language. It saves a lot of time once you get the hang of it. And to be sure"—Ms. Graves pulled the boy close—"we've certainly had enough time together to practice."

Algernon puffed his bangs out of his eyes and smiled.

"I—er—" Mr. Tinker stammered. "Well, I'm sorry for your loss, kids."

"And Algernon's doll isn't a doll, by the way," Agatha said. "It's a marionette with its strings cut off. Kenny is his name—a nickname for Kenzo, a character in one of my father's puppet plays. I don't suppose you've ever heard of Professor Hiroto Kojima, master puppeteer and renowned theatrical scholar, have you?"

Lucy exchanged a bewildered look with her father.

"Of course you haven't," Agatha muttered sarcastically. "In any event, now that we've dispensed with the pleasantries, I would like to see if Blackford House is as uninspiring inside as it is out."

Mr. Tinker shifted awkwardly on his feet. "There seems to be some sort of misunderstanding—"

"Indeed there is, Mr. Tinker," said Ms. Graves. "Mr.

Snockett said nothing about any caretakers at Blackford House."

"Well—you see, I have some papers—the deed and—" Mr. Tinker stopped himself, his eyes roving apprehensively among the children. Lucy understood. Some conversations were meant only for adults.

"Look, please, all of you, come inside," Mr. Tinker began again. "You must be tired from your trip. What say we sort out what's going on after a glass of lemonade?"

Everyone agreed, and as Mr. Tinker led the others into the house, Lucy remained behind. Her head was spinning. Blackford House belonged to *her* family! The deed said so. And not only that, *Meridian* had said so, too—right before she turned wooden again in the clock. *"You Tinkers are the caretakers,"* the cat had said.

Granted, being the caretaker of a house and its owner could be two different things, Lucy had to admit. But Blackford House was no ordinary house; and deed or no deed, being its caretaker meant that you were responsible for the magic here.

Lucy gasped. The magic! What would happen if these people found out that Blackford House was magical?

For a split second, Lucy saw the future unfold all too clearly before her eyes. Blackford House, sensing that Ms. Graves and the Kojimas were bad, would evict them just as it had done to Mr. Quigley. Ms. Graves would certainly report the incident to the authorities, and then who knew what sort of people might start poking around after that—maybe even another alchemist like Mr. Quigley!

Her heart hammering, Lucy bounded inside and joined the others in the darkly paneled foyer. Much as the Tinkers had done when they first arrived at Blackford House, Ms. Graves and the Kojimas stood at the foot of the grand staircase, eyes wide and mouths open as they gazed up at the enormous cuckoo clock built into the wall of the first landing.

"Why, it looks just like Big Ben!" Ms. Graves exclaimed.

"Big Ben isn't a cuckoo clock," Agatha muttered. Lucy glanced over at Oliver, who was looking around the foyer uneasily. She could tell he was thinking the same thing. If their guests were up to no good, then surely Blackford House would evict them at any moment.

The house, however, was quiet—save for the low, steady ticking of the clock's massive pendulum.

"And are those animals instead of numbers?" asked Ms. Graves.

"Well—er—yes," stammered Lucy's father. "I've been doing some work inside, and as you can see"—he indicated his sweatshirt—"I've made quite a mess of things."

Algernon stepped up onto the staircase and began

tugging at the round end cap at the bottom of the banister.

"Algernon, stop that!" cried Ms. Graves. "What on earth are you doing?"

Algernon explained himself in sign language, and Agatha rolled her eyes.

"He's looking for the switch to a secret passageway," she said. Algernon nodded and signed again. "A house like this is sure to have a secret passageway, he says."

Lucy exchanged an anxious glance with Oliver, and then their father chuckled awkwardly.

"Please forgive him," Ms. Graves said. "I'm afraid Algernon can be somewhat . . . *impulsive* at times."

Mr. Tinker again chuckled awkwardly. "Oh, that's all right," he said. "Anyway, follow me to the kitchen. For the lemonade, I mean."

"Very well, Mr. Tinker," said Ms. Graves.

"Please, call me Charles."

"Very well, then. *Charles.*"

Lucy sighed and folded her arms. She didn't like this new wrinkle in things at all. And to make matters worse, just before the others disappeared past the staircase and into the butler's hallway, Lucy saw something she disliked even more.

It was Samurai Kenny. He seemed to be watching her.

And he was definitely *not* smiling.

# TWO

# WHAT A MESS

Oliver stood in the library doorway, keeping an eye on the Kojimas while at the same time trying to eavesdrop on the adults in the adjoining parlor. They were sitting side by side on one of the antique sofas with a bunch of papers spread out before them.

"So, you see, Ms. Graves—"

"Please, Charles, call me Bedelia."

"Er—*Bedelia*. Well, you see it says right here in the original deed that, if the owner of Blackford House dies and no heir is found, then the house shall be bequeathed to its caretaker. We thought the owner was Mortimer Quigley and—"

"This Quigley fellow," Ms. Graves interrupted. "He's the gentleman who hired you to fix the clock?"

"That's right. He said he purchased the house from a relative of the Blackfords in England. However, once we checked things out at the town hall, there was no record of Blackford House belonging to *anyone*. And since we'd been taking care of things—well, that's how the deed came to me. My name's right here, see?"

Ms. Graves gave the deed a quick scan and then set it down among the other papers. "I don't understand," she said. "Why would Mr. Quigley hire you to fix a clock in a house that didn't belong to him?"

Mr. Tinker fumbled for a reply and then shrugged.

"And where is this Mr. Quigley now?" asked Ms. Graves, and Oliver's father fingered the collar of his sweatshirt.

"Er—well—" he stammered, "he just sort of . . . disappeared." Ms. Graves raised an eyebrow. "Believe me, I know it sounds suspicious, but—it seems Mortimer Quigley was involved in some shady dealings and—well, who knows what he was really up to and where he went. . . ."

Despite his beating around the bush, Oliver thought his father was doing a good job of explaining things to Ms. Graves without lying too much. Mr. Quigley *was* involved in some shady dealings—but no one needed to know that it was alchemy, or that Edgar Blackford and the Shadow Woods were responsible for his death.

"Forgive me, Charles," said Ms. Graves, "but this whole thing seems highly irregular. Mr. Quigley's disappearance notwithstanding, look here"—she shuffled some papers— "this is a copy of the last will and testament of Esther Snockett Blackford, who was grandmother to the twins and married to a distant relation of Roger Blackford. The will clearly states that Blackford House shall be . . ."

Oliver didn't need to hear much more to get the gist of things. Both the Tinkers and the Kojimas had a solid legal claim to Blackford House. Besides, it was hard to pay attention to the details, what with Agatha close by. Even now, as she stood with her back to him on one of library's rolling ladders, Oliver couldn't take his eyes off her.

"It's a dream come true!" she said, gazing up at the bookshelves. "Uncle Oscar would never let us in *his* library. And look at this"—she snatched a book off its shelf—"a complete set of *The History of the Decline and Fall of the Roman Empire*. Amazing!"

As Agatha thumbed through the book, Algernon sniffed the contents of one of the chemical jars on the bookshelf and smiled. He set the jar on the table, rattling some beakers among the chemistry equipment there. One half of Oliver was worried that Algernon might break something, but the other half felt sort of relieved to have other people around. Oliver couldn't imagine what it must be like for Algernon not to be able to speak. Ms. Graves had told Pop that it was the result of nerve damage. If Algernon even tried to whisper, his vocal folds would spasm, choking off his air. A very rare condition, the governess added. The poor child.

"Yeah, this room is pretty cool," Oliver said, pushing up his glasses. "We don't know much about all that chemistry stuff, though. Been meaning to learn more about it but, you know, we don't have internet here. No cable either and the cell service stinks—except for out in the truck, I mean."

"Who needs all that when you've got a whole universe

of books at your fingertips?" she said. "Or a pair of giant windows."

Agatha giggled. She was referring to Kenny. Algernon had set his samurai puppet on the window seat so that its big, bulging eyes appeared to be gazing out at the Shadow Woods beyond the pasture.

The Shadow Woods.

They weren't nearly as scary as when Oliver first moved in, he thought, and they were a lot smaller, too. The clock was responsible for that. It shrank the Shadow Woods back to their normal size after they'd nearly taken over the house. Still, Oliver thought Kenny would look right at home there. With his broken nose and messed-up hair, the puppet looked more like a zombie than a samurai. His face was white and smudged with dirt, and his thick, arching eyebrows made him look angry.

Oliver turned his gaze back on the adults. Despite the fact that they were talking about serious stuff, there was also something about the way his father was acting around Ms. Graves that Oliver had never seen before. He seemed sort of nervous, but in a shy, smiley way that—

"*Hell-ooo?*" Agatha said, snapping her fingers.

Startled, Oliver blinked back at her with a look of, Huh, what?

"I asked you a question." Agatha hopped off the ladder

and moved closer to the painting of Roger and Abigail Blackford above the library's hearth. "Who are they?"

Oliver glanced back at his father, who, at precisely the same moment, pointed to the painting above the parlor hearth and began stumbling over a fib about where it came from. That was one of the first magical things the house did after the clock was fixed—it painted a portrait of the Tinkers, hung it above the parlor hearth, and moved the Blackfords' portrait to the library. Deed or no deed, if there was ever proof that the Tinkers were the rightful owners of Blackford House, their portrait was it.

But how could Pop ever explain such a thing to Ms. Graves without giving away the house's secrets?

"Well?" Agatha asked, and Oliver stepped farther into the library.

"Er—that's Roger and Abigail *Black*-ford," he said, voice cracking, and he cleared his throat.

"Right, our long-lost twentieth cousins and whatnot," Agatha said dully. "Do you know what happened to them?"

Oliver shrugged. "Well, from what Pop found out at the town hall, Roger Blackford died first. About forty or fifty years ago, I think. Abigail died later. She was over a hundred years *old*."

Oliver cleared his throat again—ugh, stupid voice cracking!—but Agatha didn't seem to notice. She just hugged her elbows, her eyes never leaving the painting.

"Anyway," Oliver went on. "Pop said that, after the old lady died, the house stood empty for like thirty years. Mr. Quigley—the guy who hired us to fix the clock—he told us that he was the owner. But that was a lie and . . . well, you know."

Oliver swallowed hard and pushed up his glasses. He was sounding like an idiot.

"They look like zombies," Agatha said, jerking her chin at the painting. "And that black spot—what, was there a fire here or something?"

Oliver shrugged awkwardly. He'd thought the same thing when he first arrived. The Blackfords' skin was gray and their eyes almost black, and in Abigail's arms was a large, smoky smudge, as if the paint there had been burned away. But Oliver knew now that the smudge used to be a portrayal of Edgar Blackford as an infant. There was another smudgy painting of Edgar as a boy upstairs. The house was responsible for marring his image, just as the house was responsible for the portrait of the Tinkers in the parlor.

But there was no way Oliver was going to tell Agatha all that.

Just then, a gentle hissing sound came from the chemistry table. It was Algernon. He'd mixed something in one of the beakers and now it was foaming over!

"Algy!" Agatha snapped, rushing to his side. "What do you think you're doing?"

Algernon made some quick hand gestures, but Agatha waved him away just as quickly. Oliver could sense the boy's frustration as he frowned and hung his head.

"You'll have to forgive him," Agatha said, turning to Oliver. "He wants you to know that he's a very good chemist. He's won awards"—Agatha swiveled her eyes back to Algernon—"but that's no excuse for messing with things that don't belong to you."

Algernon made a fist and, looking up at Oliver, rubbed it on his chest in a circle. Oliver figured the gesture meant "sorry."

"Er—it's no biggie," Oliver said, his eyes on the beaker. The foam was now spreading out all over the table. "Let me go grab a rag or something."

Oliver dashed through the parlor and out into the foyer, where he spied Lucy staring up at the painting of Blackford House in the adjoining dining room. Oliver knew what she was up to—she was looking for a sign of Ms. Graves and the twins. He'd done the same thing earlier, while the others were finishing their lemonade in the kitchen. As far as Oliver could tell, nothing had changed. His family was still on the porch, waving to the young man atop the carriage, and the white horse was still grazing in the pasture.

Impulsively, Oliver hurried around the other way, through the butler's hallway, and into the kitchen, where he searched under the sink for some rags and came up empty. Pop must've used them all in the clock, he thought, and was about to run up there when Lucy entered from the dining room. Their eyes met, and Oliver felt caught.

He'd been trying to avoid her.

"I thought you were Pop," Lucy said, and an awkward silence passed between them. Oliver wasn't mad anymore about the fight with Billy, but given the mess Algernon had made in the library, he wanted to keep Lucy out of it. She'd been acting weird for a couple of weeks now—sort of grumpy and distant all the time—which was why he'd let her tag along with him and Billy. Big mistake that was.

Lucy looked down at the floor and said, "I really am sorry about Billy."

"Just forget about it, okay?" Oliver said, turning to go— he needed to find those rags before the whole library was full of foam.

"If you want to hang out with him," Lucy said quickly, "you know, just the two of you at the parade, I mean—I won't bug you guys."

Oliver had forgotten about that. Tomorrow was the big Watch Hollow parade, which commemorated a famous battle from the Revolutionary War. It was a huge deal around here—huger than the Fourth of July, Billy had told him. Billy's father was even going to dress up as Ben Franklin and march with the Merchants' Guild.

Oliver fumbled awkwardly for something to say—Lucy really was sorry, he could tell—but then Agatha peeked in from the dining room and things got even more awkward.

"Oh, there you are," she said, stepping inside. "Change of plans, I'm afraid. Whatever was foaming there in the library has now stopped and turned to powder. I should think a dustpan and brush will suffice."

Lucy met Oliver's eyes as if to say, What is she talking about? But Oliver just pushed up his glasses and cleared his throat.

"I knocked over one of the beakers on the chemistry table," he lied. "It must've reacted to something and—well—it made a mess in there."

Now Agatha met Oliver's eyes questioningly, but he just retrieved a dustpan and brush from the broom closet. He motioned for Agatha to follow, and then a soft crackling sound came from somewhere behind him. Oliver whirled. On the counter was a large fruit bowl that only moments

34

ago had been empty. But now it was filled with jelly beans!

"Oh, how wonderful!" Agatha exclaimed. "I'd been so focused on other things, I didn't even notice you had my favorite candy of all time!"

Oliver and Lucy gazed at each other in disbelief. They had seen some strange things during their two months in Watch Hollow, but this was the first time Blackford House had made candy appear out of thin air. And all for Agatha!

"May I?" she asked. His heart hammering, Oliver nodded; and as Agatha grabbed a handful of jelly beans, he looked over at Lucy. Her lips were trembling and her eyes were moist. Oliver knew what she was thinking—Blackford House had actually *welcomed* Agatha—but before he could figure out what to do about it, Lucy burst into tears and stormed out the back door.

"What's gotten into her?" Agatha asked through a mouthful of candy, but Oliver just shrugged back at her like an idiot. Agatha appeared to consider this for a moment, then moved to the door and stared outside.

"Who are we kidding," she said, folding her arms. "Your sister's upset about losing her home. Understandable, given all you've been through. I overheard your father explaining to Ms. Graves. Your mother—she's been gone two years now?"

Oliver heard himself say, "Uh-huh," but his mind was racing a mile a minute. If Blackford House had welcomed Agatha with a bowlful of candy, then maybe it knew something that they didn't. Maybe the Kojimas belonged here after all!

"Life can be cruel, indeed," Agatha said—more to herself, Oliver thought. "Best not to get too attached to things— people, places, and whatnot. Never know when they'll be taken away from you."

Oliver's stomach twisted. Maybe it was because Agatha was looking outside, but there was something in her tone that reminded Oliver of how Teddy, aka Edgar Blackford, used to speak to him at the edge of the Shadow Woods. Sad, distant, always a double meaning, always knowing more than he was letting on—like when he duped Oliver into using the acorn dust that both cleared up his acne and gave him the nightmares.

Oliver gulped and pushed up his glasses.

"Then again," Agatha said, turning back to him with a smile, "I suppose only time will tell."

Agatha held out her hand for the dustpan and brush, and Oliver gave them to her.

"Right, then," she said. "Let's clean up that mess."

As Agatha slipped out through the door to the dining room, Oliver's eyes fell again on the bowlful of jelly beans.

His heart was still pounding, and his feet felt rooted to the spot.

"Yeah, what a mess," Oliver said to himself.

And somewhere in the back of his mind, he heard Teddy agree with him.

# THREE

# GUESTS, SOME WELCOME, SOME NOT

"*L*ucy!" Oliver called again from the house, but Lucy just hugged her legs closer and buried her face between her knees. She wasn't crying anymore, but her cheeks were all sweaty and her butt was sore. The carriage house's big double doors were open, but the air inside was stuffy and stale. Lucy had been sitting there for half an hour. Maybe longer.

"*All right, then. Suit yourself!*" Oliver shouted, and Lucy heard the back door slam. Her stomach squeezed, and a lump rose in her throat. What a baby she was, hiding out like this. So what if Blackford House had welcomed Agatha? Pop was still the rightful owner—Lucy was just sure of it!

Lucy raised her head and peeked out from around a stack of boxes. Most of the stuff they'd moved from the city was stored in here now, along with the electric generator and the camping equipment they'd had to use when they first arrived in Watch Hollow. That had been two months ago; but now, especially with the arrival of Ms. Graves and the Kojimas, it seemed like another lifetime.

What happened? Blackford House was supposed to have been what Lucy had always dreamed of: a big house with giant windows and a room of her own—never mind that it was a *magical* house. And for the first couple of weeks, life here in Watch Hollow *had* seemed magical. But gradually, Lucy felt things begin to change; and then one day, it

40

seemed, she woke up and the magic was gone.

It was more than just the clock animals. Lucy missed her friends back home. Didn't help either that Blackford House was way out in the boonies and there were no kids around. Back home, everything had been close; and during the summer, there were always kids to play with at the park—not to mention swim camp at the Y and Lucy's soccer league. Lucy had been their best goalie, but now that bully Betty Bigsby would probably take over.

Just then, Lucy heard her father's old pickup sputter to a start. Lucy leaped to her feet and dashed out of the carriage house, but her legs were stiff and achy, and by the time she made it around front, Pop was already halfway down the driveway. And there was Ms. Graves's BMW following him. Where were they going?

Lucy bounded up the porch and inside the house. "Ollie?" she called, her voice echoing in the foyer. "Hello? Is anybody here?"

Nothing—only the low ticking of the clock at the top of the stairs.

Lucy hurried through the dining room and into the kitchen, where she found a note scribbled in marker on the message board that used to hang in the clock shop.

*Dear Lucy. Went into town to find out who owns the house. Ollie*

"So they just left me?" Lucy cried. Her eyes darted to the bowl of jelly beans on the counter, and she smeared off the note with her hand. Lucy frowned. She'd left a big smudge of grime on the message board. Her hands were filthy from being outside all day, and the rest of her felt all gross and sweaty from hiding in the carriage house.

Lucy made a beeline for the bathroom in the servants' wing, where she washed up and rebraided her hair. "Frog-face," she said to herself in the mirror, then stuck her tongue out at her reflection and shuffled back to the kitchen. This was shaping up to be the worst day ever—not to mention she was on her own for lunch. Lucy was fetching a loaf of bread and some peanut butter from the pantry when she noticed the fruit bowl again.

It was no longer filled with jelly beans but piled high with bright red apples!

"What the—?" Lucy sputtered, and then she heard the distant whinny of a horse outside. Lucy rushed to the door and gasped.

About fifty yards away, standing by the fence on the near side of the pasture, was a beautiful white horse—and not just any horse, but the white horse from the painting in the dining room!

Lucy's heart began to hammer. She had seen the mysterious horse in person only twice before—once, galloping

42

around the pasture the morning after they fixed the clock; and the second time, grazing at the edge of the Shadow Woods on a rainy afternoon two weeks ago. Pop said that it was probably just a coincidence—that the horse was more likely from a farm nearby—but deep down, Lucy knew different.

Instinctively, Lucy stuffed a bunch of apples in the crook of her arm and slipped out the back door. She moved quickly at first and then slowed down as she drew closer to the pasture. The horse just stood there like a statue. The animal's muscular body gleamed like polished marble, and its long white mane looked as soft as silk.

Lucy hardly dared to breathe—the horse had never let *anyone* in her family get this close before. And sure enough, as Lucy reached the fence, the animal tossed its head back and shrank away.

"It's all right," Lucy whispered, and she offered the horse an apple through the fence. The horse nickered, shook its slender neck, and began pawing nervously at the grass. Lucy made a shushing sound, and the horse stopped, pricking its ears forward and cocking its head.

"Go ahead," Lucy said, nudging the apple. "I just want to be friends."

The horse lowered its head, took a few steps toward her, and then stopped with its quivering nostrils only inches above her hand. Lucy felt as if her heart would explode with excitement—she could actually feel the warmth of the animal's breath on her fingers.

"That's it," Lucy whispered—when for no reason the horse swung its head violently away. Lucy gasped, and a tense silence followed in which she didn't move a muscle. The horse didn't move either, and just stood there with its ears pitched back and its eyes fixed on the house. Lucy opened her mouth to speak, and then the great beast reared, shrieking and striking out at the air with its forelegs.

Lucy screamed and staggered back, dropping the apples, and the horse bolted away from her across the pasture.

"Wait!" Lucy cried, but the horse just kept charging forward, and a moment later, it was gone in the Shadow Woods.

Without thinking, Lucy picked up one of the apples, slipped between the fence rails, and ran across the pasture. She reached the edge of the Shadow Woods in a matter of seconds and skidded to a stop. The horse had disappeared down a dark, tunnel-like path that was littered with leaves—but Lucy dared not follow.

"Hey, horse, you still there?" Lucy called, breathless and shaking, but there was no sign of the animal anywhere. Lucy tossed the apple into the gloom, losing sight of it at once, and a second later, she heard it land with a *thump* on the leaf-strewn path. Lucy listened, hoping for a sign that the horse was still there, but all that came from the woods was a moaning breeze that rustled the leaves and brushed at her bangs.

Lucy's spine prickled, and she backed away. At the same time, a thick, knotted tree root bulged up from the ground where she'd just been standing. Lucy froze with her heart in her throat. The root twisted and turned a bit, then shriveled and sank back beneath the ground. Lucy exhaled with relief.

The first and last time Lucy had gone into the Shadow Woods was on the night she and Fennish rescued the clock animals from the Garr. And even though the Garr was dead now and the balance here restored, Pop said there would always be tension between Blackford House and the Shadow Woods. That's the way balance worked, he explained: with equal tension on either side. Lucy wasn't quite sure what he meant, only that she had no desire to go into the Shadow Woods ever again. Not even for a horse.

Lucy heaved a heavy sigh and walked back toward the house. She wasn't scared anymore. And even though the horse had run away from her, Lucy felt better than she had before. The house had given her the apples so she could make friends with the horse. Oh yes, Lucy was certain of it. And everyone knew that when someone gave you a gift, the polite thing to do was to say thank you.

"Thank you," Lucy said, gazing up at the house, and it was then that she noticed a shadowy figure watching her from the library. The way the light was hitting the windows, Lucy couldn't tell for sure who it was—only that someone had stayed behind in the house and hadn't answered when she'd called!

Lucy ran back inside and into the library, where she found Samurai Kenny sitting on the window seat with his back to her. Algernon must have left him there when they went into town. Lucy's cheeks grew hot.

"Get away from my windows!" she cried, knocking the puppet to the floor. In the next moment, Lucy felt bad, and she picked up Kenny and sat him in one of the big leather armchairs near the hearth.

"I'm sorry," she said. "But those are my windows and I don't want you and your family here."

Samurai Kenny just stared back at her with his bulging bug eyes, and all at once Lucy felt like an idiot. What the heck was she doing yelling at a puppet? And yet, there was something about the way Kenny was looking at her now that she liked even less than him sitting in her windows. Maybe it was a trick of the light, but the samurai's eyebrows seemed to be slanting down more and his mouth looked frownier than ever.

Lucy's skin crawled, and her heart began to hammer. In the two months since they defeated Edgar Blackford, Lucy had never felt scared to be alone in Blackford House—not even at night in her room upstairs. Sure, sometimes she felt sad, even when staring out her ten-foot-tall windows. But now, being alone here with Kenny—

Just then, the sound of a car horn startled her. Lucy squealed and ran into the parlor. She kneeled on one of the antique sofas and, parting the curtains ever so slightly, gazed out the window. A small moving van was pulling up in the driveway.

"Oh no," Lucy muttered, and she ducked down out of sight. The van, no doubt, was here to deliver Ms. Graves's and the Kojimas' stuff!

A tense few seconds passed in which Lucy heard the van's engines shut off, followed by footsteps on the porch and the gong of the doorbell—not once, but twice. Lucy crouched down lower on the sofa and squeezed her eyes shut—*Go away, go away!* she wished as hard as she could— but instead, the man outside telephoned Ms. Graves. There was some back and forth about what to do, and then the man began unloading the van onto the porch.

Lucy's heart sank, and she buried her face in a throw pillow. The man was done in less than five minutes, and then Lucy heard the van pull away. Lucy immediately ran outside and found a dozen or so boxes stacked neatly on the porch. There was also a large travel trunk with Ms. Graves's name on it. Lucy drew her foot back to kick it, but then stopped herself and slumped down miserably in one of the wicker armchairs.

A short time later, the others returned, and Lucy's father explained that there wasn't anyone at the town hall who could help them—not today, anyway, what with everyone getting ready for the parade and all. They would have to try again on Monday, but even then, Pop said, they might still have a long road ahead of them.

The rest of the afternoon was somewhat of a blur. Lucy and Oliver helped move the boxes into the foyer, but because they still hadn't figured out who was the house's rightful owner, Ms. Graves didn't feel comfortable unpacking just yet. She had insisted on staying at a hotel, but Mr. Tinker wouldn't hear of it, and it was decided that Lucy and Oliver would sleep in her room, the Kojimas would bunk in Oliver's, and Ms. Graves would take Pop's room while he slept downstairs in the servants' wing.

"But I count *four* bedrooms up here," Agatha said. The children had just finished settling in and stood in front of the one room in Blackford House that no one dared enter.

Edgar Blackford's bedroom.

Agatha tried the doorknob, but it was locked.

"We don't go in there," Lucy said, and Agatha asked her why not. Lucy looked to Oliver for help, upon which he stammered a bit and pushed up his glasses.

"It's still a mess," he said finally. Agatha shot Algernon a suspicious glance, but he just puffed his bangs out of his eyes and shrugged.

"You Tinkers are just full of secrets, aren't you?" Agatha said, and then the twins hurried down the servants' staircase to the kitchen.

Technically, Lucy thought, Oliver had told the truth. After the house was restored, Edgar Blackford's bedroom was the only room that remained the way it had been when the Tinkers first moved in—dusty, its wallpaper peeling and faded. All the furniture and toys were still covered with sheets, and last Lucy had seen, the black, smudge-faced painting of Edgar was lying facedown on the floor. No one knew why the room hadn't changed, but since it once belonged to an evil alchemist, the Tinkers thought it best to stay out.

Lucy and Oliver stood in front of the door a moment longer, and then Oliver hurried downstairs after the Kojimas. Lucy had wanted to apologize for the way she'd acted earlier—including hiding in the carriage house and not coming when he called—but she didn't know how. With everything that had happened that day, things just felt awkward.

And later, at supper, things got even more awkward. Mr. Tinker made some hamburgers on the grill, but despite his attempts at small talk, their guests didn't say much—not even Agatha. And during dessert, Algernon kept nodding off. Ms. Graves apologized on his behalf—they were still on London time, she explained. Lucy didn't know what that meant. After all, they were in Rhode Island now.

"I should've liked some jelly beans for dessert," Agatha said out of nowhere, and she pushed her fork lazily at her pie. "There were loads of them there in that bowl on the counter before we left for town. I wonder what happened to them."

Agatha fixed her eyes into Lucy's, and Lucy felt her cheeks go hot. Agatha was accusing her of taking her candy!

A tense silence passed as Lucy looked to Oliver and her father for help—but they just went on eating their dessert. Did *they* think she'd taken Agatha's jelly beans, too? Lucy hadn't told them yet about how the house made the apples appear for the horse—and she certainly wasn't about to tell Agatha—so Lucy kept her mouth shut.

Just then, a firecracker exploded outside in the distance.

"A prelude to the big show tomorrow night," Lucy's

father said, nodding at the window—he was trying to lighten the mood, Lucy could tell. "Bigger than the Fourth of July around here."

"Oh yes, the Battle of Watch Hollow," Agatha said wearily. "I read all about it. Nearly two hundred and fifty years ago, a band of Rhode Island militiamen, outnumbered and outgunned, defeated an entire British regiment. Inconsequential in the war as a whole. But then again, it seems people around here do love their petty victories."

Agatha flashed a smile at Lucy across the table and then dug into her pie. Lucy glared at her—she was so mad now she couldn't have explained what really happened to the jelly beans even if she'd wanted to—and then another firecracker exploded outside. This one louder.

"Probably an M-Eighty," Oliver said quickly—he was trying to lighten the mood, too, Lucy thought. "They're like a quarter stick of dynamite. And they're illegal around here. This kid we know, Theo Bigsby? He's a real jerk. He got caught selling M-Eighties in school back in Massachusetts and got ex-*pelled*."

Oliver's voice cracked on *pelled*, and he cleared his throat. A tense silence passed, and then Algernon yawned.

"I'm afraid we should be getting to bed," said Ms. Graves, rising, and Lucy's father also rose to be polite. "We can't thank you enough for your hospitality and"—Ms. Graves regarded Lucy sympathetically—"well, thank you again for having us."

Even though she hadn't done anything wrong, Lucy suddenly felt guilty on top of being mad. And as Ms. Graves and the twins disappeared up the servants' staircase, a lump the size of a coconut lodged itself in Lucy's throat.

Mr. Tinker suggested Oliver accompany their guests to make sure they found their towels and stuff. Oliver obliged, and as Lucy and her father went about cleaning up the kitchen, she kept waiting for him to start lecturing her. But Pop didn't say a word—not because he was upset, Lucy understood, but because he still didn't know quite how to talk to her (even though he'd been trying harder lately). And for once, Lucy was grateful.

It was all she could do to keep from crying.

Soon, it was dusk, and Lucy found herself sitting on the porch steps alone. Fireflies danced in the distance by the river, while crickets and the occasional faraway pops of firecrackers filled the air. She didn't feel like crying anymore, nor did she did feel like talking when her father came out a short time later.

"You doing all right?" he asked, sitting down beside her, and Lucy shrugged.

"Funny, huh?" he said after a moment. "Of all the strange things that have happened since we moved here . . .

somehow today seems the strangest."

"You mean, because of them?" Lucy asked, not looking at him.

"Yeah . . . *them*," her father said dramatically, but Lucy didn't think it was funny. Mr. Tinker cleared his throat. "Anyway—I wanted to talk to you about—"

"I didn't take those jelly beans!" Lucy blurted, bursting into tears, and she told her father everything—how the apples just appeared in the fruit bowl, how the horse just appeared in the pasture, even how she hid in the house when the moving van came. And when she was finished, Lucy's father put his arm around her and held her close.

They sat like that for a long time; and once Lucy stopped crying, her father gave her a squeeze and whispered, "Everything's going to be all right. I promise."

Lucy's father kissed her on the cheek and went to bed. A short time later, Lucy was in bed, too, but sleep seemed farther away than the distant pop of the firecrackers outside. Even so, it felt good to be bunking again with her brother, even if things were still weird between them. Oliver hadn't said much before bed; and once the lights were out, he'd just sort of grunted good night and rolled over with his back to her.

Was he still mad about Billy? Oliver wasn't one to hold a grudge, so maybe he *did* think she'd taken Agatha's jelly beans. Or maybe he was just worried about losing Blackford House. Heaven knew that was all Lucy could think about.

Lucy closed her eyes and imagined her windows in the library. Yes, they were still *her* windows no matter what, and just thinking about them made her forget that Ms. Graves and the Kojimas were down the hall. At least for a little while. Soon, however, her thoughts drifted down to the window seat—and who was sitting on it.

Samurai Kenny.

Lucy squeezed her eyes tighter and tried to push the creepy-looking puppet from her mind. But every time she imagined her windows, Samurai Kenny was there, too.

Lucy's eyes snapped open, and she rolled over to face her brother. Oliver's back was to her, his body just a big gray lump under his sheet in the moonlight, but Lucy could tell by the sound of his breathing that he was asleep.

"Ollie?" she whispered just to be sure, but there was no response—only the crickets and a soft breeze rustling the leaves outside.

Lucy gently wiggled around so that her head was at the bottom of the bed and her feet at the top. This was how they'd had to sleep back home in the clock shop, when the bed she and Oliver shared was too small to lie in normally. Lucy's bed here in Blackford House had more than enough room for the two of them—a big four-poster with a canopy and everything—but she thought sleeping the old way might make her feel better. And it did for a little bit, but in the end, it just wasn't the same.

Lucy closed her eyes and tried to imagine that Torsten was lying beside her. He always made her feel better, especially when she was feeling scared and lonely—like on that first night here in Blackford House. Lucy didn't feel as scared now as she had back then, but she was definitely as lonely.

Maybe even lonelier.

# FOUR

# A CHANGE IN
# ATMOSPHERE

Lucy awoke early the next morning to the smell of frying bacon. It was cloudy outside and Oliver was gone.

Lucy slipped off her nightgown and threw on a pair of shorts and a T-shirt. She then hurried down the hallway into the bathroom, where she quickly brushed her teeth and wove her hair into its customary single braid. Her stomach was growling like crazy—Lucy had been so miserable the night before, she'd hardly eaten anything.

Lucy padded down the servants' staircase and into the kitchen. Everyone was already gathered at the table except Ms. Graves, who was busy cooking.

"Finally," Agatha muttered under her breath, and Lucy gave her a dirty look.

"Er—good morning, sunshine," said Mr. Tinker, pulling out Lucy's chair. She sat beside him and sniffed. Aftershave. Lucy raised a questioning eyebrow.

"I'm afraid I knocked over a bottle of Old Spice in the bathroom," her father said, chuckling nervously, and Lucy rolled her eyes.

Ms. Graves set down a glass of orange juice in front of Lucy. The governess was dressed in a pair of khaki shorts, a linen blouse knotted at the waist, and her red hair was pulled back in a ponytail. Lucy might have thought she was an entirely different person if not for the red-jeweled pendant around her neck.

"I hope you don't think me presumptuous," said Ms. Graves. "But since I was up early, I thought the least I could do was cook breakfast."

And what a breakfast it was! There were waffles, scrambled eggs and bacon, and some biscuit-like things called scones.

"I can't take credit for these," said Ms. Graves, putting them on the table. "Your father surprised me this morning, although he tried to play innocent."

His eyes never leaving the scones, Lucy's father again chuckled nervously. Lucy understood. The scones were in the fruit bowl, which meant *the house* had made them appear—just as it had made the jelly beans and apples appear the day before!

Lucy looked over at Oliver to see what he was thinking, but he was just staring down at his plate, eating quietly.

Soon the conversation turned to the day ahead, and it was decided that Ms. Graves and the twins would join the Tinkers at the parade. Oliver looked up from his plate in shock, but he didn't say anything—nor did he say much after breakfast, when everyone piled into the truck. The adults sat up front, and even though it looked like rain, the children rode in back in the open bed.

Once they were across the narrow river, the woods quickly gave way to rolling farmlands and fieldstone walls rushing past. Lucy's attention, however, was on Algernon, who was sitting in the rear of the truck, gazing off at the road behind them. Lucy wondered if he missed Kenny. Algernon had wanted to bring him to the parade, but Ms. Graves wouldn't allow it—for the same reason she hadn't allowed him to bring Kenny into town the day before.

"This is a new start for us, Algernon," she'd said. "And you don't want to make the wrong impression should you meet any other lads your age."

After a short distance, Lucy had the sense of first going up and then going down, and all at once, it seemed, they were at the edge of town. Everything was decorated in swags of red, white, and blue as if it were the Fourth of July.

"Not quite a thriving metropolis, is it?" Agatha muttered, and Lucy rolled her eyes. Sure, downtown Watch Hollow was a joke, but Lucy loved coming here. The narrow streets and brick and clapboard storefronts reminded her of the small town in New Hampshire where her mother had grown up.

Eventually, Lucy's father found a parking spot not far from the parade route. Everyone hopped out of the truck, and soon they had taken their places amid the crowds along Main Street. Lucy saw some girls her age, but she felt too shy to approach them—not to mention, only a freak would just walk up to someone at a parade and say hi.

"Hey, Tinker!" someone yelled, and Lucy spied Billy Mahoney across the street. He was sitting on top of a mailbox in front of his father's hardware store. Billy waved Oliver over—he didn't want to lose his prime viewing spot, Lucy could tell—and Oliver slipped out a bag of Skittles from his pocket.

"Hey, Pop, Billy left these yesterday," he said. "Okay if I give them back?"

"Sure. And why don't you introduce him to Algernon while you're at it."

Algernon smiled and flicked his bangs out of his eyes, but Oliver's face dropped.

"Er—well—" he stammered, pushing up his glasses, and Lucy understood. It was okay to hang around with Algernon at Blackford House, but out here in the real world it was a different story. Oliver was embarrassed. Or maybe, Lucy hoped, he was afraid that Billy might start talking trash. With his argyle socks, bow tie, and bangs, Algernon would be an easy target—never mind if Billy found out about Kenny.

Fortunately for everyone, the drum roll signaling the start of the parade commenced a second later, and Oliver stayed right where he was.

Soon, the street was filled with a column of people dressed in Revolutionary War costumes. First came the drummers and fife players, followed by the usual procession of clubs, firefighters, and police officers, as well as a small troop of Girl Scouts. Lucy's heart ached at the sight of them. She had never given much thought to joining the Girl Scouts back home, but now . . .

"Top of the morning, Tinker!" someone said. It was Billy's father, Lucy saw. He was dressed up like Ben Franklin and walking along with the Merchants' Guild. Lucy's father waved back at him, and as the rest of the Merchants' Guild marched past, Lucy noticed something very strange.

An elderly gentleman, dressed in black and walking behind Billy's father, stared in shock at Ms. Graves as he passed—almost as if he recognized her, Lucy thought. Ms. Graves didn't seem to notice, however, and as the Ladies' Auxiliary Fire Department marched into view, Lucy lost sight of the old man down the street.

It all happened so quickly that, when the parade was over, Lucy wasn't sure it had happened at all. A light rain had begun to fall, and as the crowds of paradegoers quickly dispersed, Lucy looked for the old man but couldn't find him. And yet Lucy was certain she had seen the old man before. He had sort of a pointy chin, high cheekbones, and longish white hair. But Lucy couldn't tell if he was bald like most old guys because he'd been wearing one of those stupid tricorn hats.

A few minutes later, everyone was back in the truck; and by the time they returned home, Lucy had forgotten about the old man altogether. The light rain had become a downpour and she was soaked. Lucy and the other children hurried inside to change, while Mr. Tinker took off for Narragansett to pick up some clam cakes and chowder for lunch. Their guests had never eaten that kind of stuff before.

"I saw how Oliver behaved," Agatha whispered, stopping Lucy in the foyer as the boys headed upstairs. "You saw it, too, when your father suggested he introduce Algy to his friend at the parade. Oliver was embarrassed."

Lucy's stomach sank. "Er—well—" she sputtered. "Billy's kind of a jerk and—"

"I'm used to not having any friends," Agatha said. "But it still stings when I see it happening to Algernon. So, as long as we're here, I'll promise to stay out of your hair if you promise to help me avoid situations like that going forward. Deal?"

Lucy nodded dumbly—she wasn't sure what she was agreeing to—but as her eyes followed Agatha up the stairs, Lucy felt ashamed of her brother. What a jerk! Hopefully,

Algernon didn't pick up on it, too—never mind, what good was having a friend like Billy if you always had to worry about being embarrassed in front of them?

And speaking of friends, Lucy found it hard to believe that Agatha didn't have any. Yeah, she was a nerd, and probably took all sorts of grief for that. Not to mention, she was a snot, too. But nerds and snots had other nerds and snots for friends, didn't they?

Lucy bit her lip. Maybe under different circumstances, she wouldn't mind having Agatha as a friend. She was super smart—way smarter than Lucy—and prettier, too. No one had ever called Agatha Kojima a frog-face, Lucy was willing to bet. Moreover, she looked out for her brother. And Lucy had to give her props for that.

Lucy sighed and hurried up to her room. Everyone had called dibs on the bathroom, so she was the last to finish changing. And while Oliver and the twins retreated to the library, Lucy sat down on the porch to wait for her father.

Hope the pickup doesn't leak, she said to herself—or worse, break down. It was raining so hard now that Lucy could barely make out the clumps of trees down by the river. As for the Shadow Woods, Lucy couldn't see them at all.

It was then that, gazing off in the direction of the pasture, Lucy spied the shadowy figure of a man standing beneath an old oak tree about fifty yards away near the fence. Lucy stood up and moved to the railing to get a better look, when a gust of wind blew a thick sheet of rain across her field of vision. Lucy blinked, and in the next moment, the shadow was gone.

Lucy gulped, and her heart began to hammer—just a trick of the light, she decided at once—but suddenly, she had no desire to be out here on the porch by herself. Nor did she have any desire to hang with the others in the library when she slipped back inside. So instead, Lucy climbed up the stairs to visit with the clock animals. She hadn't spoken to them at all since their guests arrived, and quickly brought them up to speed on everything that had happened. Lucy knew that they could still see and hear her, even if they were in such a state that they couldn't respond.

"Don't worry, Torsten," she whispered, squatting down in front of him—the little dog lived near the floor in the *six* hole. "We're not going anywhere. We're still the caretakers here, no matter what these people say. Right, Fennish?"

Lucy scratched the top of Fennish's head—the one-eyed rat lived in *seven* hole with his patch facing outward. Lucy hoped he could feel her, even if he couldn't see her.

"I really miss you guys," Lucy said, backing away so Meridian could get a better view of her from her *twelve* hole, and then the cuckoo doors swung open and Tempus

Crow shot forward. His squeaky mechanical beak opened with a *"Caw!"* for one o'clock, and then the dark wooden bird disappeared back inside.

"That's some clock, isn't it?" said Ms. Graves, and Lucy whirled to find her standing on the stairs leading up to the second floor. How long had she been there? And had she heard Lucy talking?

Lucy gulped and stared up at the governess guiltily.

"Do you always talk to the animals like that?" asked Ms. Graves, coming down. Lucy blushed and dropped her eyes. How was she going to get out of this? There was *no way* Lucy could tell her the truth about Blackford House. Owners or not, the Tinkers were the caretakers, and it was their job to protect the magic here.

"It's nothing to be ashamed of," said Ms. Graves, joining Lucy by the clock. "I, too, had more than my share of imaginary friends when I was a child."

Lucy lifted her eyes and Ms. Graves smiled at her sympathetically. Under any other circumstances, Lucy would've felt like an idiot to be accused of having imaginary friends at her age. And she *did* feel like an idiot—kind of—but better feeling like an idiot than having to tell the truth.

"In any event, the clock is a wonder," said Ms. Graves, gazing up at it. "Your father tells me it generates electricity for the entire house."

Lucy thrust her hands in her pockets and shifted uncomfortably on her feet. "Oliver's the expert on all that. And Pop. They can explain it better than I can."

"But neither of them is here," said Ms. Graves, fingering her ruby pendant, and Lucy took a deep breath.

"Well," she began, "the clock is what's called a perpetual motion clock—which means it never needs winding. Most perpetual motion clocks run on changes in atmosphere. But this perpetual motion clock is powered by those animal statues. They're made up of shadow wood and this stuff called sunstone. The whole house is, as a matter of fact. But the animals—well, they're kind of like the clock's batteries."

Lucy pointed at Frederick, the turtle who lived in the *five* hole.

"Anyway, there really is no such thing as a perpetual motion clock," Lucy went on. "Sometimes, the energy runs out." This was where she needed to be careful. She couldn't tell Ms. Graves that the clock stopped before because Mr. Quigley brought Edgar Blackford back from the dead. So, instead, she just said, "That's why Pop is working so hard on the fail-safe. It's almost done. He just has to test it out."

Ms. Graves smiled and moved to the mechanical room door. "For someone who claims not to be an expert, you sure sound like one to me."

Lucy shrugged and smiled bashfully. "Well, I guess it sort of rubs off on you."

Ms. Graves opened the mechanical room door and peered inside. Even though it was still raining, there was plenty of light coming from the porthole in the back wall.

"Good heavens," she said, gazing around at the machinery. "I took the twins on a tour of Big Ben once, but it was nothing compared to this. Look at all these gears and pipes. And is that the fail-safe mechanism?"

Ms. Graves was pointing to a pair of steel extension arms that arched down from the ceiling and hovered like claws just outside the swing range of the pendulum.

"That's part of it, yeah," said Lucy. "I'm not quite sure how it works, but you see that iron ball in the middle of everything? That's called the conductor sphere. It's where the energy from the sunstone and the shadow wood mix together to power the clock. Pop's fixed it so the conductor sphere powers the fail-safe, too. I think."

"Ingenious," said Ms. Graves. "Your father is something, isn't he?"

"Well, he's been working on it day and night ever since we got here. He keeps promising us we'll go to the beach and do other stuff, but . . ."

Lucy bit her lip and looked at the floor.

"All work and no play makes Charles a dull boy, eh?" said Ms. Graves.

Lucy shrugged, and the governess lifted Lucy's chin with her finger.

"Tell you what," she said, holding her eyes. "Weather permitting, how about I take you and the others to the beach tomorrow? We'll make a regular day of it, just the five of us—that is, unless your father dares to come along."

Lucy's face brightened, and she nodded excitedly.

"Now, run along and join the others," said Ms. Graves. "And if your father's not back in half an hour with our clam cakes, we shall hound him incessantly on that ancient cell phone of his until he returns."

Lucy giggled and moved to the stairs.

"How ingenious indeed," Ms. Graves muttered, peeking again into the mechanical room. Lucy was about halfway down the stairs when suddenly the governess let out a bloodcurdling scream.

Lucy spun around and ran back upstairs. Ms. Graves was gone, she registered in one moment, and in the next, an explosion of red light from the mechanical room nearly blinded her. Springs boinged and gears clanked— something was wrong with the clock, Lucy realized with mounting horror. And Ms. Graves was inside!

Blinking floaters from her eyes, Lucy froze in the mechanical room doorway. Instead of Ms. Graves, the floaters dissolved around a ten-foot-tall monster. It had the head of a bull, the upper body of a human, and legs that were a combination of both!

Lucy nearly fainted with fright, and then the monster let loose a deafening roar and lunged for her. Lucy screamed and fell backward onto her bottom—but the mechanical room door was too small for the monster and it got stuck. Lucy tried to scramble away, but then the monster squeezed itself out and lunged for her again. Lucy threw up her arms to protect herself—she was sure she was a goner—when without warning, Meridian and the other animals leaped out of the clock!

Teeth gnashed and claws slashed as the clock animals swarmed the monster and drove it away from Lucy. The monster roared and tore the animals from its body, flinging them squealing through the air.

"Don't hurt them!" Lucy cried.

And then she was falling, tumbling backward down the stairs.

# FIVE

# ENTER THE LABYRINTH

Startled, Oliver dropped his book and went rigid in the library's big leather armchair. Had someone just screamed?

"That sounded like Ms. Graves," Agatha said, leaping up from the window seat, and Algernon stopped what he was doing at the chemistry table. Oliver heard the muffled *boing* of springs and metal clanking—something was wrong with the clock, he knew at once—and then a deafening roar shook the walls, followed by a *different* scream.

"Lucy!" Oliver cried, and with his heart hammering, he dashed from the library to the parlor. Squeals and growls and more of that horrible roaring filled the air, and then Oliver nearly tripped over Lucy as he ran out into the foyer. She was lying on the floor at the bottom of the stairs.

Oliver cried out for her, and then something roared at him from above. Oliver whirled, and came face-to-face with a hulking, red-eyed monster staring down at him from the top of the stairs. Oliver thought it had horns like a bull, but it was hard to tell for sure in the shadows.

Oliver froze in terror, vaguely aware of Agatha's screams behind him, and then the floor tilted sharply, and they were rolling together toward the center of the foyer. Algernon and Lucy crashed into them a split second later, and then the walls began to rotate and push inward all around. The chandelier retracted into the gloom overhead, and a half dozen or so flaming torches swiveled out of the walls.

Oliver could hardly believe his eyes. He staggered to his feet as the floor leveled out again and the last wall slid into place, blocking off the staircase and the monster entirely. Its roars sounded farther away now, and in the next moment, Oliver heard the monster's thundering footsteps trailing off deeper into the house.

The others stood up and gazed around in stunned silence. In each of the foyer's four dark-paneled walls there was now an entrance to a flickering, torch-lit hallway.

"What on earth is going on?" Agatha cried. "The house—it's transformed!"

Algernon looked around and hugged Kenny tight. And for a split second Oliver wondered where the puppet had come from—Kenny hadn't been with them in the library—and then Lucy leaned on her brother for support.

"Lucy, are you all right?' Oliver asked.

"She's fine!" Agatha snapped, her eyes wide with panic. "But the house—is this your idea of a sick joke or something? And where is Ms. Graves?"

Oliver ignored her and asked Lucy what happened. Lucy rubbed her temples and shook her head, trying to remember.

"I don't know," she said groggily. "One minute I was talking to Ms. Graves, and the next, she was screaming in the clock. There was this flash of red light and I . . . I tried to save her but . . . the monster. It must've gotten her."

"You mean Ms. Graves is—?" Oliver couldn't bring himself to say *dead*, but Lucy understood just the same. She choked back a sob and nodded.

Oliver moaned in despair and turned to the twins, who were now just standing there in shock. Lucy, however, must have mistook it for something else, because all at once she went from sad to angry.

"Wait a minute," she said. "How do we know *they're* not behind all this?"

Oliver opened his mouth, but nothing came out. It was all too much. There was a monster upstairs and Blackford House had . . . *changed*—but Agatha and Algernon were just standing there stone-faced as if nothing had happened.

"Everything was fine until they showed up," Lucy went on, her voice trembling. "How do we know they're not trying to dupe us like Mr. Quigley did?"

Oliver fumbled for something to say, but Lucy didn't give him the chance.

"Don't you see? They came to Watch Hollow for the same reason as Mr. Quigley. They know about the magic here!"

Oliver gasped and shook his head—Shut up, Lucy! he was trying to say—but Lucy just ignored him and moved closer to the twins.

"Only Ms. Graves didn't know what she was messing with either," she sneered, clenching her fists. "I bet Ms. Graves was an alchemist, too. I bet she brought that thing up there back from the dead or something—just like Mr. Quigley did to Edgar Blackford. Only this time, the monster killed the alchemist right away!"

Oliver's head was spinning—he couldn't believe what Lucy was saying—when without warning, Algernon threw Kenny down and tackled Lucy to the floor for bad-mouthing Ms. Graves. The two of them wrestled there a moment, arms flailing and yanking at each other's hair, and then somehow, Oliver and Agatha managed to pull the children apart and onto their feet.

"Stop it!" Agatha cried, and Algernon burst into tears. "Stop it, I say! Now, more than ever, we must keep our heads—regardless of what these people think!"

And with that Lucy burst into tears, too. Oliver wasn't sure what to do—it was taking every ounce of his strength not to panic—so he picked up Kenny and handed him to Algernon. But still, the boy would not stop crying. Agatha shook him by the shoulders.

"Pull yourself together!" Agatha cried, and then Algernon began gasping for air. "No, don't try to speak—just breathe! *Breathe!*"

But Algernon *couldn't* breathe, Oliver understood. His condition—what Ms. Graves had told Pop. Algernon's vocal folds were in spasm and choking off his air!

Oliver watched helplessly as Agatha held her brother's face in her hands. "Look at me," she said calmly. "I'm still here. I'm not going anywhere, but I need you to stay with me. I need you to *breathe.*"

And with that Algernon's throat opened and his chest swelled with a big snatch of air. A few seconds later, he was breathing normally again. Oliver exhaled with relief. Algernon was okay. And not only that, he'd stopped crying.

"That's it," Agatha said, thumbing the tears from her brother's cheeks. "Ms. Graves would want us to carry on. There will be time to mourn her after we get out of this place. And we *are* getting out." Agatha took her brother's hand and turned to Oliver. "I don't know what's going on here, but if you'll kindly point us toward the exit, we'll be on our way."

"Please," Oliver said. "Something very bad has happened here. We don't know what or why but—"

"On the contrary. Given your sister's talk of magic and alchemists, clearly you Tinkers know more than you've been letting on. Come along then, Algernon. We'll find our way out of this madhouse on our own!"

Oliver didn't say a word as Agatha quickly led her brother around the foyer to each of the four doors. And at each of the doors she found the same thing: a torch-lit hallway leading deeper into the house.

Agatha turned back to Oliver and, with trembling lips, said, "Very well then. If you plan on killing us, then I suggest you get on with it." Agatha raised her fists. "Keep in mind, however, that my brother and I shan't go down without a fight."

Despite his fear, Oliver's heart ached for her. Agatha was doing her best to be brave, but she was just as terrified as he was.

"No one's killing anybody," Oliver said. "You have to believe us. We're just as scared and confused by all this as you are. Right, Lucy?"

Her head hung low, Lucy dragged her wrist under her nose and nodded.

Agatha folded her arms and, tilting her head back, regarded Oliver suspiciously. A tense silence passed as Oliver fumbled for what to say, and then he pushed up his glasses and exhaled anxiously.

"I'm sorry we didn't tell you before," he said. "But our family—well, we're the caretakers of Blackford House. It's our job to protect the magic here." Agatha's eyes darted around fearfully. "I know it sounds crazy but—well, look around you. Blackford House is *magical*. But something's wrong now. Nothing like this has ever happened before!"

"But that monster," Agatha said, her voice shaky. "And Ms. Graves—"

Just then, the monster roared from somewhere deep within the house. Everyone flinched, and then Oliver heard the unmistakable sound of a cat screeching. Lucy gasped.

"Meridian!" she cried, hurrying over to one of the hallways, and then Torsten yelped and began to whimper. Oliver's heart nearly stopped.

The clock animals were alive!

Lucy dashed across to another of the hallways and cried out for Torsten, but Oliver just turned around in place—he couldn't tell where the animal noises were coming from. More roaring, and then Torsten stopped whimpering.

"Torsten, where are you?" Lucy cried, and then she turned to Oliver. "The animals are alive, Ollie!"

"What the—?"

"They saved me from the monster," Lucy said, cutting Oliver off. "But Torsten sounds hurt! We've got to help him!"

Oliver's head was swimming. If Torsten and Meridian were alive, then that meant the clock had stopped. And if the clock had stopped, then that meant the Shadow Woods would start creeping toward the house again!

Oliver glanced over at Agatha, who was just staring back at him, eyes wide and mouth hanging open. Too much was coming at her at once—Algernon, too, Oliver could tell. The twins didn't know about the clock animals, but now hardly seemed like the time to explain—not to mention, Oliver had no idea how Torsten and the others could come alive during the *daytime*. That was not the way the magic worked here!

"Ollie, did you hear me?" Lucy said, clapping her hands to get his attention. "We need to find Torsten!"

Oliver just stood there blinking back at her like an idiot. He didn't know what to do. Blackford House had changed, a monster had killed Ms. Graves, and now the clock animals were alive during the day. The whole world was going crazy!

"Come again?" Agatha said, and Algernon frantically signed something, ending with a gesture that looked like rabbit ears. "What do you mean you saw a rabbit?"

"Nessie Three!" Lucy cried, and then Algernon snorted like a pig. "And Reginald Eight! Where, Algernon—where did you see them?"

Algernon pointed up at the ceiling and then made a bouncy gesture with his hand.

"Up on the landing, before the house changed," Agatha translated.

"They're two of the clock animals!" Lucy said, and Agatha gaped back at her in confusion. "There's no time to explain! Torsten's in trouble! You heard him, he needs our help!"

"You're mad if you think we're going after some dog," Agatha said. "We need to get out of this insane asylum before that monster kills us, too!"

Lucy looked at Oliver to back her up, but all he could do was swallow hard and push up his glasses. "Ollie, say something!"

"Agatha's right," he muttered. "There's a monster here and the house is going bonkers. There's no telling what will happen next."

Lucy's lower lip began to tremble, and tears of betrayal pooled in her eyes. Oliver's heart twisted—he hated Lucy looking at him that way—and yet he knew deep down that Agatha was right. Blackford House was too dangerous now and Torsten could be anywhere. Better if they got out and ran for help.

But before Oliver could explain, Lucy took off down one of the torch-lit hallways.

"Lucy, wait!" Oliver cried out after her, but she kept going. Oliver looked helplessly at the twins, and then everyone followed, catching up with Lucy around an unexpected corner.

Oliver's chest grew tight with panic. Lucy was leading them down what looked like a torch-lit version of the upstairs hallway—only it *kept going*, turning sharply every twenty yards or so, and there were no bedrooms.

"We need to get out of here," Agatha whispered over her shoulder to Oliver. The twins were walking ahead of him now, and Algernon was carrying Kenny in such a way that his eyes, flickering with torchlight, looked just as scared as everyone else's.

"But this is impossible," Oliver said. "Blackford House isn't this big!"

"Well then, it's clearly gotten *bigger*," Agatha said. "Please, Lucy, let's just turn around and go back to the foyer. That's where the front door used to be. For all we know, it might be down one of those other hallways."

"We're not going anywhere without Torsten!" Lucy cried.

Oliver groaned. Something very, *very* bad was happening—something even worse than the last time the clock stopped. Blackford House had not only gotten bigger, it had also unleashed a monster. But how? And why now? Ms. Graves was in the clock when everything happened, so could Lucy be right? Was the governess an alchemist like

Mr. Quigley? And did she accidentally bring that monster back from the dead?

Oliver shook the thought from his mind and pushed up his glasses. He refused to believe it. Blackford House would've never let Ms. Graves inside if she were like Mr. Quigley—same for the monster—which could mean only one thing:

The monster was already here.

Oliver's chest grew so tight he could barely breathe. They had been living in Blackford House for only two months, but could there have been *another* monster besides the Garr hiding here the entire time? And what if it was hiding now, waiting to ambush them around the next corner? Even worse, what if there were more than one?

"Agatha's right," Oliver said. "We should head back to the foyer and look for the front door."

But as usual, Lucy didn't listen to him, and soon she led everyone into another torch-lit chamber like the foyer. There were more hallways branching off from it, but there was also a door. Lucy hurried over and pressed her ear against it, listening for what seemed like an eternity, and then she tentatively curled her fingers around the knob.

"Be careful, Lucy," Oliver whispered. "The monster might be waiting for us on the other side."

The twins backed away, ready to run, and then Lucy slowly opened the door.

Oliver gasped.

It was Edgar Blackford's bedroom.

And there, hanging on the wall in a shaft of flickering torchlight, was his smudgy-faced portrait.

# SIX

# NEW ENEMIES

Lucy dared not breathe as she reached into the darkened bedroom and tried the light switch. Nothing happened.

"Torsten?" Lucy whispered, peering tentatively inside. As far as she could tell, nothing had changed since the last time she saw Edgar Blackford's bedroom; but still, in the flickering torchlight streaming in behind her, the room looked like a gathering of ghosts. The bed, the furniture, and Edgar's old rocking horse were still covered in sheets. Shadows danced on the walls. And the portrait . . .

Lucy gulped. The portrait of Edgar Blackford was hanging on the wall now, whereas before, it had been lying facedown on the floor. And not only that, the image of Edgar looked *darker*, as if the smoky black smudge that covered his face had spread out over his entire body.

The back of Lucy's neck prickled. This was not good.

"I don't like this," Oliver said, echoing her thoughts. The others had gathered behind her, blocking most of the torchlight, and Lucy could now see a thin, glowing crack between the window curtains on the far side of the room.

The window!

Lucy rushed over and flung the curtains open—but where the window should have been, there was now only a step up into yet another torch-lit hallway.

Lucy cried out in frustration and whirled back to the

others, who were still huddling close together just outside the door. More torchlight was flooding into the bedroom now from the window, and as Lucy caught sight of the terrified look on Oliver's face, it was all she could do to keep from losing it.

"We need to get out of here," he said. "This room is no place for us."

Looking around fearfully, Agatha pulled her brother close. Lucy's guts twisted with guilt. She shouldn't have said those horrible things to them. The twins were just as scared as she was—not to mention, they had just lost Ms. Graves. Lucy couldn't imagine how they were keeping it together.

"The dog is not here," Agatha said flatly. "Now may we please go back to the foyer and look for the door?"

"Wait—what an idiot I am!" Oliver said, consulting the combo compass-wristwatch-flashlight he always wore, and then he moved toward the window. "The front door is on the south side of the house. And south is in this direction."

Agatha and Algernon stepped eagerly into the bedroom. "Of course," Agatha said. "We can use your compass to lead us out!"

"But what about Torsten?" Lucy said, moving back toward the door. "He must be this way, down one of the other hall—"

"Do *not* run off again!" Agatha snapped, and Lucy froze. "Thanks to you, we're even more lost than before. From now on, please let cooler heads prevail."

Her anger rising, Lucy looked to Oliver for help, but her brother just swallowed hard and, glancing down again at his compass-watch, moved closer to the window.

"Agatha's right," he said. "We need to keep our heads so we can get out of here."

"But what about Torsten?" Lucy cried. "How can you just abandon him?"

"We won't be good to anyone if that monster finds us first," Oliver countered.

Furious, Lucy clenched her fists and gritted her teeth. This was the second time Oliver had betrayed her!

"Lucy, please listen," he began again. "Blackford House is like a maze now. We're lost and there's a monster here. It's not safe for us anymore. If we can get out and find help, maybe we can—"

Oliver was cut off by the bedroom door slamming. Everyone jumped, and then Lucy rushed over and tried the doorknob. "It's locked!"

The walls began to creak and groan, and Lucy heard a horrible ripping noise coming from across the room. At first, she thought the flickering shadows were playing tricks on her, but then her eyes put it together.

The portrait.

The image of Edgar Blackford had come to life and was tearing itself away from the rest of the painting!

Screaming, everyone rushed for the window and jumped up into the hallway. Lucy glanced back over her shoulder and froze, watching in horror as Edgar leaped from the painting onto the bed. In the orangey torchlight, he looked like a walking shadow—two feet tall, entirely black, and flat like the canvas from which he came!

The shadow Edgar bounded to the floor and, with a horrible growl, tore the sheet off the rocking horse. The animal came to life at once—its eyes bulging, its lips curling back over its hideous wooden teeth. Edgar leaped up onto the horse's back and yanked the reins, upon which the animal reared up off its rockers and, with a deafening whinny, charged!

Lucy shrieked and took off down the hallway at a full sprint. Oliver and the others were way ahead of her now, but the thundering gallop of hoofbeats was approaching fast behind her. Lucy glanced back over her shoulder—the shadow Edgar and his horse were only a few yards away—and then Lucy tripped and went sprawling onto her hands and knees.

Lucy flipped over. At the same time, the rocking horse whinnied and leaped for her. Lucy screamed and threw up her hands to protect herself, when one of the torches in the wall spewed out a jet of fire and set Edgar and his horse ablaze. A great whooshing sound filled the hallway, and then just like that, Edgar and his horse were nothing more than a heap of ashes on the floor.

Lucy staggered to her feet. A second later, the others came rushing back.

"What the heck?" Oliver cried, and Lucy blinked around in disbelief. The torch burned normally again, and the ashes were swirling upward and dissolving into the air before her eyes.

Heart hammering and breathless, Lucy explained what had happened. Oliver pushed up his glasses and gazed up at the torch. The twins, shaking with fright, held each other close. Even Samurai Kenny looked afraid, Lucy thought.

"What is going on here?" Agatha cried, her voice trembling. "How could those *things* just come alive like that?"

Oliver shrugged. "Nothing like this has ever happened before," he said. "Not even when the Shadow Woods took over!"

"What do you expect from an evil alchemist's bedroom?" Lucy said, starting off again. "Come on, we need to keep moving."

But no one followed. Oliver was splitting his gaze between the torch and the floor. All that remained of Edgar and his horse was a black stain on the rug.

"But don't you see, Lucy?" Oliver said. "None of this should be happening. Whatever is causing all this—the monster, I don't know—well, it should've never been able to get inside in the first place."

"What are you talking about?" Agatha asked.

"Blackford House can sense when people are bad. That's why Mr. Quigley hired us. The magic here was weak because the clock had stopped, but still, once the house realized what Quigley was up to, it kicked him out and wouldn't let him back inside."

"Why are we talking about all this now?" Lucy said. "We need to keep moving before more evil stuff comes out of that bedroom!"

Suddenly, Lucy heard a deep scraping sound behind her. She spun around and *thud!*—a stone wall slid into place, sealing off Edgar Blackford's bedroom farther down the hallway. Lucy gulped.

"Well, that solves that problem, doesn't it?" Agatha said—she didn't look so scared anymore, Lucy thought. "However, before we go forward, I have a confession. As my body is still on London time, I was up before anyone else this morning. I went down into the library, and what should I stumble upon but Roger Blackford's journal."

Lucy gasped and exchanged a horrified glance with

Oliver. It had never occurred to them to hide Roger Black-ford's journal. What a pair of idiots! The journal was all about alchemy, and basically said flat out that the house was magical!

Agatha moved to the wall and touched its high, dark paneling. "Blackford talks at length about his experiments with sunstone and shadow wood, and how the balance of their energies powers the clock. He also talks about the house being sentient, but I must confess, I didn't think he meant literally. In any event, let me guess: Mr. Quigley raised Edgar Blackford from the dead, and then Edgar blackmailed him into recalibrating the clock to run off shadow wood so he could live here. I'm sure I'm missing some details, but that's the gist of it, am I correct?"

Lucy's mouth hung open. "How did you know?"

"I listen," Agatha said. Lucy was at a loss. Agatha must be even smarter than she had thought. But still, that didn't make Lucy like her any better.

Oliver cleared his throat and pushed up his glasses. "That is gist of it, yeah," he said. "But when *you* arrived, the clock was working normally. The magic here was strong and the monster should've never been able to get inside in the first place. Unless—"

"It had been here all along," Agatha said, the light dawning, and Oliver nodded.

"That's what I've been thinking, yeah," he said, pushing up his glasses.

"But that's impossible!" Lucy cried. "We've been living here for two months. I think if there was a monster here this whole time we'd have known about it!"

"But, sis, it's the only thing that makes sense."

"Something must've happened when Ms. Graves went into the clock," Agatha said, thinking. "She must have released the monster from someplace unknown to you. A hidden chamber, most likely. You know, with a secret lever or—"

Agatha stopped herself, and her eyes flashed anxiously at Lucy.

"What?" she replied.

"Well, forgive me," Agatha said hesitantly, "but, from what I understand, your father hadn't tried his fail-safe yet, correct?" Lucy nodded. "Well, do you think it's possible that *Ms. Graves* might have tried it—perhaps even accidentally—and in doing so, somehow transformed the house and released the monster?"

Lucy looked at Oliver uneasily.

"Well, did she?" Oliver asked her, but Lucy only stared back at him like an idiot. She couldn't remember exactly what had happened. Everything now seemed fuzzy in her head.

"In any event, the monster is here," Agatha said. "It killed Ms. Graves and, for whatever reason, Blackford House can't evict it. Best then to just accept that fact and move on."

Algernon snatched in a quick breath and began breathing deeply. Oliver, on the other hand, looked as if he had stopped breathing altogether. He just stood there, eyes wide and mouth gaping. His mind was racing a mile a minute, Lucy could tell. If Ms. Graves threw the fail-safe, causing all this to happen, then that meant Oliver and Pop were somehow responsible. Obviously, the fail-safe hadn't worked—the clock had stopped ticking—but what if it did something else? What if it caused all *this*?

Either way, Lucy thought, Agatha was right about one thing: Blackford House wasn't strong enough to kick out the monster now. And that was a terrifying thought in and of itself. If the house with all its magic couldn't stop the monster, how would they?

"What are we going to do?" Lucy asked.

"Let's just try to get out of here," Oliver said quietly.

As the children moved down the hallway, the walls began to creak and groan all around. At the same time, the monster roared somewhere in the distance. Without meaning to, the children huddled close—except for Algernon, who moved to the wall and pressed his hand against it.

"What is it?" Agatha whispered. Algernon signed something and then motioned for her to join him. Agatha did, and ran her hand along the dark paneling. "Yes. It's as if you can feel the house straining." Agatha nodded at Lucy and Oliver. "Go ahead, see for yourself."

Lucy tentatively touched the wall. Agatha was right. Lucy could almost feel the wood contracting beneath her hand. She nodded for Oliver to try, but he just ignored her and checked his compass-watch instead.

"Let's keep moving," Oliver said.

And with that the children hurried down the hallway, keeping close together, with Oliver in the lead. Eventually, the hallway turned sharply—then it turned again, and again, and not long after, the floor sloped upward and the hallway narrowed and began to twist at odd angles. Often, the monster could be heard roaring far away, upon which the house would creak and groan, and more stone walls slid into place, forcing the children down hallways that hadn't been there only seconds before.

"Stupid compass," Oliver kept muttering to himself. Lucy thought it was useless to keep checking it when they had no choice where to go. But still, she didn't say anything.

Eventually, Oliver led them down a hallway that looked very different from the others. There was only one torch at the entrance, and a few yards beyond that, the shadow wood paneling abruptly stopped and the hallway became all stone with a dead end. The children were about to turn back, but then the floor rumbled, and the dead end slid open to reveal a narrow flight of stone stairs curving upward into darkness. Oliver flicked on the flashlight in his compass-watch.

"Do you think the house is trying to lead us somewhere?" Lucy asked.

Oliver shrugged and, aiming his light ahead of him, stepped onto the stairs.

"Hang on," Agatha said, and Lucy turned to see Algernon pointing to the wall. "What are you saying?"

Algernon tucked Kenny under his arm and made some rapid hand signals.

"You're right," she said. "The stone here is different."

"What are you talking about?" Lucy asked.

"Up until now, this maze has been composed of sunstone and shadow wood, both structural elements original to Blackford House"—Agatha rapped her knuckles against the wall—"but I don't know what sort of stone this is."

Just then, the floor began to rumble again, and the stone wall that had opened only moments before began sliding back into place.

"Hurry!" Lucy cried, and the twins crowded into the

stairwell just as the wall closed behind them with a *thud!*

Lucy just stood there for a moment, breathless and blinking in the narrow, spiraling shaft, and then Oliver turned off his watch light.

"Listen," he whispered, and Lucy heard a soft scraping sound. At the same time, her eyes began to adjust to the darkness, and the stairs took shape in some dim light spilling down from above—light that was very different from torchlight.

"Come on!" Oliver cried, and the children followed him up the winding steps to a room bright with daylight. Lucy squinted as she looked around. They were in the attic—or what *used to be* the attic, Lucy realized with mounting horror. The cramped space was packed with boxes and trunks and lots of other junk, but the ceiling . . .

"It's gone!" Oliver cried, echoing Lucy's thoughts, and her knees nearly buckled with fright. Where the ceiling once had been, there was now a large, gaping hole that seemed to be getting larger before her very eyes. Lucy could see the sky, cloudy and gray as it had been all day. And the soft scraping sound she had heard—Lucy gasped.

It was the walls!

Yes, incredibly, the attic walls were made entirely of stone now and getting higher by the second—the large blocks multiplying one by one as is if being laid by an invisible hand!

Oliver grabbed Lucy by the arm. "We need to get out of—"

But before Oliver could say *here*, the monster exploded up from under some junk on the far side of the attic with a deafening *"ROOOOOOAAARR!"*

The children screamed, and Lucy ducked just in time to avoid an old dressing dummy that came flying at her across the room. Instinctively, she scrambled head down for the exit—but the stairwell was now sealed off!

"We're trapped!" Agatha cried.

Lucy spun around—the hulking, horned beast was coming straight for them, snorting and snarling as it climbed over a pile of trunks in the middle of the floor. In the next moment, the trunks collapsed and the monster went sprawling, its arms and legs flailing as it howled in frustration.

The children darted this way and that, crashing into one another, and then everyone began backing away, keeping close, until they hit a wall. The monster rolled off the heap of crumpled trunks and stood to its full height, throwing back its head with another earsplitting *"ROOOOOOAAARR!"*

Lucy squeezed her eyes shut and threw up her arms,

ready for the worst—when without warning, the wall gave way behind her and she fell backward.

Lucy's eyes snapped open just in time to catch the monster rushing toward her, and then the wall swung shut again, plunging the children into darkness.

# SEVEN

# OLD FRIENDS

The monster pounded furiously on the wall, and Lucy threw up her arms to protect her head. She was lying on her back in the dark, certain that at any second the wall would come crashing down on her. But then the monster roared one last time and Lucy heard its thundering hoofbeats trailing away. A moment later, everything was still and silent.

"Is it gone?" Agatha whispered.

Oliver flicked on his watch light and Lucy blinked around. They were lying next to each other in one of Blackford House's secret passageways. Lucy could tell by the old-fashioned lathwork in the walls. Normally, Lucy hated being in the secret passageways. They were dark and narrow and smelled weird. But now, Lucy wouldn't have traded lying here for a beach in the Bahamas.

Lucy turned her head to look around and the base of her skull began to throb. She'd whacked herself good when she hit the floor, but only now was the pain kicking in. And the secret passageway smelled weirder than normal—sort of like sour milk.

Lucy turned her head the other way, and discovered the smell was coming from Kenny. Algernon was lying stiff as a board beside her, and Kenny's creepy samurai face was so close that Lucy could have kissed it.

"Blech!" Lucy uttered, squirming away, and the children rose shakily to their feet. Lucy sighed with relief. They were all there, all of them safe and sound.

"I should've known," Agatha said, dusting herself off. "That's not just any monster, but a Minotaur."

"A Minotaur?" Oliver asked. "You mean, like from ancient Greece or something?"

"Ancient *Crete*, to be precise. From what I remember, the gods wanted to punish the king of Crete for something or another, and his wife ended up giving birth to the Minotaur. The king had the labyrinth built as a place to hide his son—a place where the Minotaur could live but not escape."

"You mean like a prison?" Lucy asked.

"Or a home, depending on your perspective. The labyrinth protected the Minotaur just as much as it protected everyone else from it." Agatha looked around. "I should've put it together before. Blackford House is not just becoming a maze, but a *labyrinth*. After all, what's a labyrinth without a Minotaur? The two must be connected!"

Algernon hugged Kenny close and began to breathe deeply. He was terrified. They *all* were. Not only was there a Minotaur lurking around, but also, Blackford House was transforming itself into a home for it. Lucy had seen the labyrinth taking shape in the attic with her own eyes!

"Wait a minute," Lucy said, the light dawning. "Do you think the Minotaur is doing the same thing Edgar Blackford tried to do? You know, changing the house into a place where it can live? Only instead of changing it from the outside, the Minotaur is changing it from the *inside*?"

"I suppose it's possible," Agatha said, and Algernon quickly signed something. "Then again, Algernon says the labyrinth seems to be getting in the Minotaur's way just as much as ours. Clearly, it's sentient, like the house, so perhaps Blackford House is creating this labyrinth as a *prison* for the Minotaur. Like in the myth."

Oliver pushed up his glasses and looked around. "But if Blackford House can transform itself into a labyrinth," he began, "why didn't it do so before? You know, when Edgar Blackford tried to take over?"

Algernon shrugged and then signed a reply.

"Edgar Blackford wasn't a Minotaur," Agatha translated. "Perhaps the monster is too strong for Blackford House to evict. So, it's doing the opposite. It's imprisoning it."

The others seemed to consider this, but Lucy shivered at the idea. If Blackford House was becoming a prison for the Minotaur, did that mean it was becoming a prison for them, too?

Just then, a deep creaking sound came from the attic side of the passageway. Oliver swept his watch light toward it, and Lucy discovered that the wall that had shielded them from the Minotaur was made of sunstone bricks. And the creaking was coming from inside.

Agatha pressed her palm against the wall. "The wall is vibrating. You can feel it!"

Lucy placed her hand against the wall. Agatha was wrong. The wall wasn't just vibrating, it was *shaking*—like Pop's old electric generator but without the noise.

Oliver swallowed hard. "We should get out of here before this wall changes, too."

"Aye," a voice replied from the shadows, and everyone jumped. Oliver swung his watch light around, and a single eye twinkled up at Lucy from the shadows at her feet.

"Fennish!" Lucy cried, squealing with joy, and she scooped up the rat into her arms. "Oh, how I've missed you!"

Lucy hugged and kissed him. Fennish was warm, and Lucy could feel the beat of the rat's heart against her chest. "But how did you find us?"

"The smell of fear is strong," Fennish said flatly, and Agatha pulled her brother close. The twins looked terrified, but Lucy couldn't help but giggle. She was so used to being around talking animals, she'd forgotten that the rest of the world wasn't.

Lucy quickly introduced Fennish to the Kojimas, and

then Oliver asked him what was going on. The rat heaved a raspy sigh and leaped from Lucy's arms.

"Once again, an evil presence is trying to take over Blackford House," he said, moving toward the darkened passageway. "Only this time, from the *inside*."

"So I was right!" Lucy exclaimed. "The Minotaur *is* making a home for itself!"

"More like something is making a home for the Minotaur. A dark magic has come to Blackford House. I've seen it with my own eye—a creeping darkness that infects everything it touches. It's transforming the house into a labyrinth, and the objects inside into . . . well, I don't know what they are."

"The rocking horse," Lucy said. "It came alive when the painting of Edgar Blackford touched it!"

"Then you've seen the infection, too," Fennish said, and everyone nodded—except for Algernon, who began signing something.

"Algernon wonders if this is some sort of elaborate defense," Agatha translated. "You know, could the Minotaur have brought this dark magic here and Blackford House is trying to imprison it? After all, the labyrinth did save us."

Fennish shook his head. "The labyrinth didn't save you. It was *the house*. Blackford House is using all its power to fight the dark magic and protect us. But now that the clock has stopped, I fear the labyrinth is winning."

"Of course," Oliver muttered. "The attic is at the top of the house."

"What does that have to do with anything?" Lucy asked.

"We learned in science that, when a tree dies, it dies from the top down. Perhaps it's the same for Blackford House." Oliver shone his watch light on the wall of sunstone. "That's why the labyrinth had completely taken over the attic except for this one wall. Blackford House is dying from the top down—which means its magic would be the weakest here."

Fennish considered this. "Then I suggest we head for lower ground."

"Fennish, do you know where Torsten is?" Lucy asked, suddenly frantic. "We heard him earlier. He sounded hurt!"

Fennish was about to answer when a loud *crack*, like splitting timber, echoed through the passageway. Startled, everyone whirled, and Oliver trained his light again on the wall of sunstone. Lucy gasped.

A large crack was snaking its way down the mortar lines in the middle of the wall. And not only that, on one side of the crack the sunstone bricks were dissolving before Lucy's very eyes into the same kind of blocks she had seen only moments ago in the attic. Blocks for the labyrinth!

"You see?" Agatha cried. "Mr. Fennish is right. The dark magic *is* taking over!"

"Blackford House is trying to resist its transformation into the labyrinth," Fennish said, scanning the shadows. "But the dark magic is too strong."

Another crack formed in the sunstone, more labyrinth blocks took the place of the bricks, and then the secret passageway began to rumble and shake. Plaster and lathwork crumbled to the floor, a horrible splintering noise was heard, and then the walls began to close in.

"Run!" Fennish cried, dashing off into the passageway. Oliver hurried after him, lighting the way with his watch, followed closely by the twins. Lucy was last, and shortly after she started moving, she felt a blast of air on the back of her neck as the passageway closed with a loud *crunch* in the darkness behind her. But Lucy didn't dare look back. She was so terrified, she could hardly breathe.

"Keep moving!" Fennish cried. Lucy could see him scurrying up ahead, his tail at the edge of Oliver's light. The floor heaved and shook, and the splintering noise became deafening as the darkened passageway began to narrow all around.

Agatha screamed at Algernon to run faster, and then Lucy lost sight of them up ahead in the shadows. The passageway had twisted sharply, becoming so narrow that Lucy got stuck!

Lucy cried out in terror, certain she was about to be crushed, and then Algernon grabbed her by the hand and pulled her free. Together, they ran down a steep ramp. The passageway was wider here, Lucy registered dimly, but only when the floor leveled out again did she realize the splintering and crunching had stopped.

Still, everyone kept running until, finally, Fennish led them to the secret door in the bookcase—the same door through which Lucy had escaped from Mr. Quigley two months earlier. There was even light streaming in through the bullet holes the old man had made when he shot at her.

Fennish pressed the secret lever, the bookcase swung open, and everyone poured out into the library. Meridian and Torsten were waiting for them. The room was warm and bright—there were torches everywhere and a roaring fire in the hearth—but there was no time for Lucy to even catch her breath.

"Torsten!" she cried, rushing to his side. The little dog lay moaning and breathing heavily in one of the big leather armchairs. His neck was bloody, and his eyes were closed. Meridian hovered over him, her face all worry.

"Miss Lucy," Torsten rasped, cracking open an eye. "So happy to see you one last time. . . ."

"What happened?" Lucy asked. She placed her hand on Torsten's forehead. The little dog was burning up—and he was shivering.

"The monster wounded him," Meridian said.

"But it's more than that," Fennish said, scurrying over to the library's pocket doors. "The dark magic has infected him, too. Just as it has infected the house."

Fennish nudged open the doors. Where the parlor had been, there was now another torch-lit chamber with more hallways branching off from it. And where her ten-foot-tall windows once loomed above the velvet-cushioned seat, there was the entrance to the biggest hallway Lucy had seen so far.

Lucy moaned, but there were more important things to worry about at present. She needed to help Torsten!

"Sunstone cream!" Lucy blurted, dashing over to the chemical jars in the bookcase. Yes, if only she could find some sunstone cream, Lucy could heal Torsten just as she'd healed Fennish when he escaped the Garr.

Lucy stopped—what an idiot she was! They'd used up the last of the sunstone cream to defeat Edgar Blackford two months earlier!

Lucy cried out in frustration. But then Algernon set down Kenny on the window seat and moved to the chemistry table, where he began flipping through Roger Blackford's journal. He quickly found what he was looking for and snatched an armful of chemicals from the bookcase. Jars clanked and beakers rattled, something fizzed, and before Lucy knew what was happening, Algernon had mixed together a fresh jar of wood glue. Lucy could tell right away because of the smell—and because one of the jars Algernon had used was labeled Shadow Wood Dust.

"No, you need sunstone cream!" Lucy cried, but Algernon just hurried over to Torsten and began smearing the wood glue all over his wound. The little dog twitched and moaned, and then tiny tendrils of bright purple sparkles fanned out over Torsten's neck and began stitching his wound shut.

Everyone gasped in disbelief—and then, just as quickly, the sparkles dissolved, and only a thin purple scar remained. Algernon slipped off his bow tie and bandaged Torsten's neck with it. The little dog's eyes fluttered open and he sat up, tongue lolling and tail wagging.

"Why, that feels much better," Torsten said, and he dragged his tongue across Algernon's cheek. Algernon smiled and screwed a lid on his jar of wood glue. Everyone looked at each other in amazement, and then in a rush of emotion, Lucy fell to her knees and scooped up Torsten in her arms. The little dog gave her a big sloppy kiss, too.

"Oh, thank you, Algernon!" Lucy said. "But how did you know it would work?"

Algernon signed something and pointed at Roger Blackford's journal.

"It appears someone else was up early this morning," Agatha said with a smile. Algernon gave her a thumbs-up, and then Meridian rubbed her body against Lucy's leg.

"It's so good to see you again," Lucy said, patting the cat's head. "But what about the others? Reginald and Nessie—where are they?"

Meridian exchanged an uneasy glance with Fennish. "Reginald and Nessie got away after we saved you," Meridian said. "As for the others . . . last we saw them, the monster had them trapped in the mechanical room."

"Fortunately, I escaped," Torsten said. "I tried to help the others. But as you can see, that didn't go very well."

"I was looking for the clock when I found you," Fennish said. "But the secret passageways—or what's left of them—have become a labyrinth, too."

Lucy's heart twisted. The poor animals! Were they still alive? Or had they met the same fate as Ms. Graves?

"We've yet to be introduced," Agatha said, approaching Torsten and Meridian. "My name is Agatha Kojima and this is my brother, Algernon. Might I ask if either of you saw what transpired earlier in the clock? Do you know if Ms. Graves threw the fail-safe and released the Minotaur?"

Lucy glanced over at Oliver. She could almost feel the air around him tensing.

"The red-haired lady did something," Meridian said. "I heard some metal clanking before she screamed." Oliver groaned and held his head in his hands. "But only Tempus Crow would know for certain. He was in the mechanical room when it happened. But last I saw he was still trapped in there with the others."

"But that red-haired lady wasn't there," Torsten said. "I can tell you *that* for certain."

"What do you mean?" Agatha asked.

"Just what I said, miss. Right after we ambushed it, the monster threw me and some of the others into the mechanical room. I was dashing about all over, trying to avoid the beast before I escaped. And I didn't see hide nor hair of that lady anywhere."

Lucy's stomach twisted. Poor Ms. Graves—the monster must have eaten her, she thought—but then Algernon signed something at Agatha.

"You're right, Algy," Agatha said. "Ms. Graves might still be alive!"

"Wait—what?" Lucy asked.

"The secret chamber," Agatha said. "When Ms. Graves

released the Minotaur, she might've been able to take shelter inside! We need to get back to the clock! Ms. Graves might still be in the secret chamber!"

"Secret chamber?" Fennish asked, but Agatha was already heading for the exit. Then, without warning, the library's pocket doors slid shut by themselves and the house began to creak and groan as if it were in pain. Agatha frantically tried the doors, but they were locked. At the same time, Torsten began barking up at the painting of the Blackfords above the hearth.

Lucy's heart froze.

The smoky black blob that had once been the infant Edgar Blackford had gotten bigger. And just like the shadow Edgar in the bedroom, it was struggling to get out of the painting!

"The dark magic!" Meridian cried. "Blackford House is trying to stop it from spreading!"

The blob stretched a few inches off the canvas, then snapped back and twisted and turned in Abigail Blackford's hands. Lucy could hardly believe her eyes. Abigail Blackford was actually *holding back* the blob in the painting. But in the next moment, the blob stretched out so far that it sent a vase on the mantel crashing to the hearth. Lucy and the others staggered back, and then Roger Blackford's hands slid across the canvas and grabbed hold of the blob, too. The painting shook and rattled against the wall.

That was enough for everyone, and they all scrambled up through the windows and into the hallway. Lucy was last, and as soon as she joined the others, a massive wall made of sunstone slid into place behind her and sealed off the library.

Lucy's heart was hammering—everything was happening too fast. But one thing was certain: they needed to get back to the clock to rescue Ms. Graves and the animals!

Just then, a muffled crash came from the library, startling everyone. Meridian rushed over to the wall and listened. Silence, then the sound of smashing glass and growling. Lucy's skin crawled. The blob of the infant Edgar had escaped the painting, she understood in one moment, and in the next—*boom, boom, boom!*—it began pounding on the wall of sunstone.

Meridian jumped back as a crack formed along some mortar lines running down the center of the wall. At the same time, a handful of black sunstone bricks alongside the crack dissolved into the grayish blocks of the labyrinth.

"The dark magic!" Torsten cried. "You see? It infects everything it touches!"

"Hurry!" Fennish said, making his way to the front of the group. "We need to get out of here before that wall becomes part of the labyrinth!"

Fennish quickly led them down the torch-lit hallway, with Meridian and Oliver close behind. Agatha was next, followed by Algernon, who was carrying both Kenny and his jar of wood glue. Lucy and Torsten were last.

After a short while, the floor began to slope sharply downward, and soon they came to a small square chamber filled with empty crates and wooden barrels. Racks of dusty wine bottles and shelves of old preserves lined the walls, and in one corner, dozens of shadow wood logs were stacked from floor to ceiling. Lucy's stomach dropped.

They were in the cellar.

In the flickering torchlight, across the room to her left, Lucy could just make out the stairs leading up to the kitchen; but to her right, behind a stack of crates, was another hallway like the one she was standing in.

Agatha immediately ran for the stairs with Lucy and Torsten close behind, while Oliver and the others moved toward the hallway.

"Come on, *this* way!" Agatha cried, mounting the stairs. "The clock is on the second floor!"

"Hold on, miss!" Torsten cried, hopping up beside her. "There's no rhyme or reason to this maze. The clock could be on this floor the other way!"

Lucy stopped at the bottom of the stairs. "Torsten's right," she said. "We should probably take a second before—"

"Oil!" Fennish called, cutting Lucy off from across the room. He was sniffing around the entrance to the hallway with Oliver, Meridian, and Algernon standing by.

"There, you see, miss?" Torsten said. "Mr. Tinker uses oil in the clock!"

"Which means that's the right way to go!" Lucy cried. She was about to head back toward the others when a horrible growling echoed through the cellar. Lucy whirled around.

The smoky black blob of Edgar Blackford had escaped the library and was coming fast down the hallway. And it looked *human* now—just like the shadow figure of Edgar that had chased them from the bedroom!

Lucy screamed and fell backward onto the stairs, watching in horror as the little shadow man ran at lightning speed down the hallway. The torches spewed out jets of fire, but Edgar somehow dodged them, and in the blink of an eye, he was in the cellar.

Agatha grabbed hold of Lucy under her arms and pulled her onto the stairs. Then, without warning, the cellar floor collapsed, and the little shadow Edgar—along with everything else in the cellar—was swallowed up into a big black hole.

"*AAARRRGGGHHH!*" Edgar cried, fainter and fainter as he fell—and then *splash!* everything was silent.

Lucy just sat there for a moment, heart pounding and breathless, as Torsten squeezed past her to the bottom of the stairs.

"I don't believe it," Torsten said, and Lucy joined him. The torches still burned brightly between the wine racks and shelves on the walls, but where the floor had been, there was now a wide gaping hole so deep and dark that Lucy could not see the bottom.

"It's the old cistern," Fennish said, his voice echoing in the hole. He and Meridian sat staring down into the darkness on the opposite side. Oliver stood behind them in the hallway with Algernon. Lucy exhaled gratefully. Thank heavens, they were all safe!

"Keep breathing, Algy!" Agatha yelled to her brother, and Algernon hugged Kenny and his jar of wood glue to his chest. What were they going to do now? The hole stretched from wall to wall and had to be at least ten, maybe fifteen feet wide. Lucy thought she might be able to jump it, but not without a running start—which was impossible from her position on the stairs. Then there were the wine racks and shelves in the walls—but would they hold her if she and the others tried to climb across?

Lucy swallowed back a lump in her throat as Fennish searched on his side for a board to lay across the hole. But there was nothing. Oliver suggested that Meridian and Fennish climb along the wine racks—he and Algernon could definitely make the jump if they ran, he said—but Meridian quickly nixed that idea. Not even she would dare attempt such a landing on the stairs.

"We've no choice but to split up," Fennish said. "The clock is this way, I'm sure of it, but perhaps you three might find another path—or perhaps even a way out."

"Are you mad?" Agatha cried. "I'm not leaving without my brother!"

"The infection is spreading, miss," Torsten said gently. "Blackford House won't be able to protect us forever."

There was a little more back and forth about what to do, but despite Agatha's objections, it was decided that they had to go their separate ways. The house was beginning to creak and groan again, and the hallway from the library had grown dark—the torches snuffed out. Torsten was right: the dark magic was spreading fast!

Algernon patted his heart and waved goodbye to Agatha, who, with trembling lips, cried out, "Keep breathing, brother dear! I promise, we will be together soon!"

The groups wished each other luck and then headed off

in their separate directions—Lucy, Agatha, and Torsten up the stairs; Oliver, Algernon, Meridian, and Fennish down the hallway.

"I shall not cry," Agatha muttered, sniffling as she climbed, and Lucy said the same thing.

But only in her head, so Agatha wouldn't hear her.

# EIGHT

## AGATHA

Lucy and the others had been walking for only a couple of minutes when Torsten began sniffing along the baseboard. Lucy folded her arms and looked around. The cellar stairs had brought them up into a hallway that resembled the servants' wing.

"Is it oil?" Agatha asked—she was calmer now, Lucy could tell.

Torsten shook his head. "I think it's aftershave," he said. "Old Spice, if I'm not mistaken. I'll wager this is where the bathroom used to be."

Lucy's heart squeezed. A thought had been bubbling up in her brain ever since this nightmare began, but now that she was separated from Oliver, it was getting harder to push it away. Where was Pop in all this? Had he come back from Narragansett to find Blackford House had changed? He must be worried sick about them. And what about Oliver? Would he be okay without her?

A panicky sob escaped Lucy's lips, and she inhaled sharply to snatch it back.

"Now don't you worry, Miss Lucy," Torsten said, padding over to her. "You and I have been through tougher scrapes than this. Well, maybe not *tougher*, but . . . you get where I'm going."

Torsten smiled up at her with his tail wagging and Lucy

smiled back. There was just something about the way the little dog looked at her that always made her feel better—never mind that he was still wearing Algernon's bow tie.

Lucy bent over and scratched him between the ears.

"I'm glad to see you're back to your old self now, Torsten," Lucy said. "You really gave me a scare there in the library."

Torsten hopped up onto his hind legs and licked Lucy's cheek. "Oh, it's so good to see you again, miss! I didn't realize until now how much I'd missed you!"

"Well, of course you didn't," Agatha said. "I should think you don't experience such feelings when you're in the clock, do you? Otherwise, you'd go mad."

"Er—well—I suppose you're right, miss," Torsten said. "We exist only in the present when we're in the clock."

"I suspected as much," Agatha said. "I try to live by the same philosophy, in a way. Focusing on the present does indeed help keep one's feelings in check."

"*Anyway*," Lucy said, "I've missed you, too, Torsten."

Agatha sighed wearily, and after they had pressed on a little farther, she began humming to herself. Lucy recognized the tune at once—"Dance of the Sugar Plum Fairy" from *The Nutcracker*. That had been her mother's part before she met Pop, when she was with the Boston Ballet. And often, Lucy would hear her humming the tune in the kitchen when they lived above the clock shop.

The clock shop. Lucy's heart ached at the memory of it, and in her mind, Lucy's eyes fell on her mother's old headshot hanging behind the counter. Last she'd seen it, the photograph had been on the dresser in Pop's bedroom here at Blackford House—but where was it now?

Another sob escaped Lucy's lips, this one too big to snatch back, and then Lucy burst into tears. Suddenly, more than anything, she wanted her mother. Torsten tried to console her, but it was Agatha who eventually stopped her from crying.

"Forgive me," she said. "I wasn't thinking. Please accept my apology for humming that tune."

Lucy wiped her nose and blinked back at Agatha through her tears. How did you know? she asked with her eyes.

"I know grief when I see it," Agatha said. "This morning at breakfast, before you arrived, your father told us your mother had been a ballet dancer. I should've known better. No doubt you miss her very much. I'm sorry."

Lucy dragged her arm across her cheeks and nodded. Oddly, she felt better, and after they had walked a bit farther, Lucy whispered, "I didn't take those jelly beans, you know."

Agatha looked at her sideways. Lucy wasn't sure why she'd felt compelled to speak of that right now. After all, they certainly had much bigger problems on their hands. But Lucy didn't stop there. She told Agatha about the apples and the scones, too. And when she was finished, Agatha just nodded vaguely and said, "Very well, then."

A heavy silence hung in the air as they moved on, and then Lucy asked, "What did your mom do? For a living, I mean."

"She was a chemist," Agatha said quietly. "That's where Algy gets it from. He's had a rough go of it, though. He was in the car the night of the crash."

"That's how he lost his voice, right? What Ms. Graves told us?"

"Right, but what she didn't tell you is that my brother blames himself for the accident." Lucy raised a questioning eyebrow. "Algy had been in another fight at school. The boys in his form often teased him. But this time, I gather, it was in science class. Algy threw some chemicals on one of the boys and . . . well, suffice it to say, the boy was injured and Algy was expelled. My parents went to fetch him. They were on their way back when the crash happened. Luckily, Kenny was in the car that night, or Algy might have died, too."

"Kenny?" Lucy asked.

"My father had just finished a puppetry workshop at a university nearby. Kenny and the other puppets were still in the car. I'm not quite sure how it happened, but Kenny somehow cushioned Algy's head when they crashed, and since that night, my brother refuses to part with him."

"I'm sorry" was all Lucy could say. She felt like crying again. Poor Algernon.

"I hope he's all right," Agatha said. She breathed deeply— once, twice—and then said, seemingly out of nowhere, "Uncle Oscar's mansion is much bigger than Blackford House. One needs to be careful not to get lost. That's the worst feeling in the world, isn't it? Being lost?"

Lucy nodded, even though she wasn't quite sure what Agatha was driving at.

"I don't know what we would've done without Ms. Graves," Agatha went on. "She's been the one shining light in all this. I tried my best not to get too attached to her, but I fear I let my feelings get the best of me. Some example I am to Algernon."

"Why wouldn't you want to get too attached to her?" Lucy asked.

Agatha shrugged. "If you don't get too attached to people, when they leave you, it doesn't hurt."

Lucy frowned. She wanted to tell Agatha that was a stupid way to go through life, but on the other hand, she sensed that Agatha had already figured that out for herself.

Agatha took a deep breath. "In any event, here we are,

feelings and all," she said. "I suppose we'll find our way again when we get out of here. *If* we get out of here."

"Of course we'll get out of here," Torsten said—Lucy had been so focused on Agatha, she'd forgotten the little dog was there. "And we'll rescue that Ms. Graves of yours and the animals, too. Miss Lucy is an old hand at this sort of thing. She *is* the caretaker, after all."

Lucy's stomach twisted. Some caretaker she was. She should've never let Ms. Graves go into the clock!

"We can only hope Ms. Graves made it into the secret chamber," Agatha said.

"What's all this about a secret chamber?" Torsten asked. "Far as I know, there's no secret chamber in the clock. Not even a secret passageway. You remember, Miss Lucy. That night we escaped from Mr. Quigley, the secret passageway led us to—"

"Then where did the Minotaur come from, Torsten?" Lucy asked. "You didn't by any chance happen to see it strolling into the clock, did you?"

Torsten hung his head. "Well, when you put it that way," he said glumly.

"I'm sorry," Lucy said. "I'm not trying to be mean, but how else could the Minotaur have gotten into the clock?"

Before Torsten could answer, Agatha led them around a corner, where they came upon the entrance to the dining room. Torsten padded inside a few feet, but Agatha held Lucy back by the elbow and shook her head.

"There are no torches in there," Agatha said, and Lucy understood. There had been no torches in Edgar Blackford's bedroom either. Or the attic, come to think of it.

However, there *was* light spilling into the dining room from the hallway, as well as two more hallways on either side where the kitchen and windows had once been. And just as it was for her in Edgar Blackford's bedroom, Lucy thought for a moment that the flickering shadows had to be playing tricks on her.

"What are you waiting for?" Torsten called back from somewhere to her right, but Lucy's eyes were locked on the painting of Blackford House above the buffet.

Whereas the Shadow Woods were normally just a dark smudge in the background beyond the carriage house, *now* the trees took up the entire right side of the painting. And not only that, the branches were *growing out* of the frame, fanning along the wall and down the front of the buffet, where they disappeared among the shadows under the dining room table.

Lucy's blood ran cold and her heart began to hammer. "The dark magic," she whispered. "It's spreading through the paintings!"

"We need to get out of here," Agatha whispered, and

then Torsten began barking frantically. Lucy just stood there frozen for a second, her mind unable to comprehend what she was seeing. One of the dining room chairs had sprouted a pair of wooden hands and was lifting Torsten off the floor by his bow tie!

Screaming, Lucy grabbed the chair from behind, but the chair immediately donkey-kicked her in the shin, and Lucy staggered back in pain. Torsten craned his neck and bit down hard on the chair's wrist. Something wailed like a wounded animal—but it wasn't Torsten, Lucy realized as the chair spun around. In its seat back was a pair of hollow eyes and a jagged black mouth!

"*AAAHHOOWWW!*" the mouth howled.

Everything that happened next was a blur. Lucy knocked over the chair, setting Torsten free. At the same time, the breakfront doors swung open and the dining room was a whirlwind of flying china. Everyone ducked for cover as plates and cups and saucers whizzed and shattered all around. Then Agatha seized Lucy's arm and pulled her to safety in the hallway where the windows had once been.

The girls ran, and then the floor began to rumble as if a freight train were coming up fast behind them. Lucy glanced back over her shoulder and her legs nearly buckled with fright. The dining room chairs—their wooden legs loping, their jagged mouths snarling—were chasing them down the hallway like a pack of wild dogs!

"*HELP, HELP!*" Torsten cried, darting out from under the chairs' scrabbling legs. Lucy skidded to a stop, spun around on her heels, and a second later Torsten leaped up into her arms. His whole body was shaking.

"*AAAHHOOWWW!*" the chairs howled—they were almost upon her, Lucy realized in horror—and she took off screaming again.

"Lucy, hurry!" Agatha cried. She was about twenty yards away now, standing in a doorway at the end of the hallway. Lucy pumped her legs harder. She could feel the chairs gaining fast—when suddenly, *CRASH!*

Lucy stumbled and spun around. The foyer's giant crystal chandelier had crashed through the ceiling and landed on the chairs, smashing most of them to pieces. Two of the chairs were still alive, but before they could climb over the chandelier and resume the chase, a nearby torch spewed out a jet of fire and set the chairs ablaze.

As it was for the shadow Edgar and his horse, in one moment, the chairs were flopping around in flames, and in the next, they were reduced to a heap of ashes. A thick column of smoke spiraled up into the hole the chandelier had made in the ceiling, and then the ashes dissolved, leaving only a stain on the rug.

Lucy just stood there, breathless and blinking, as Torsten

leaped from her arms and began sniffing around at the smoldering remains. A moment later, a wall of sunstone rumbled into place at the far end of the hallway, sealing off the entrance to the dining room with a *thud!*

But something *behind* her was rumbling, too, Lucy realized, and she spun around just in time to see another wall of sunstone seal off the doorway in which Agatha had been standing.

And even worse, Agatha was gone.

# NINE

# ALGERNON AND THE
# UNFORTUNATE PIG

Fennish sniffed around at the base of the wall and then looked up at Oliver.

"It is here, lad," the rat said. "I'd bet my eye on it."

Oliver sighed and glanced back over his shoulder. No sooner had they left the cellar than they came upon a doorway that had been sealed off with sunstone. Meridian and Fennish both agreed that the trail of oil continued on the other side, but for some reason, Blackford House would not let them through.

Meridian began scratching frantically at the wall. "Let us pass!" she cried out to the house. No response. Only the sounds of the torches crackling above their heads.

Frustrated, Fennish slumped back onto his hind legs, while Algernon sank to the floor with Kenny and the jar of wood glue in his lap. Oliver swallowed hard. He couldn't help feeling sorry for the kid.

"We need to press on," Meridian said, moving away from the door. "If the house doesn't want us to go this way, there's no point wasting any more of our time."

"We both agree this door leads to the clock," Fennish said. "Perhaps Blackford House is protecting us because the monster is near the clock, too."

As if to echo Fennish's point, the Minotaur roared from somewhere deep within the house. Meridian flinched, and

Fennish pressed his ear against the wall.

"Aye," he rasped. "If Blackford House is protecting us, then perhaps it will open this wall again when the coast is clear."

Meridian hissed in frustration. "But what if the coast is *never* clear?" she cried. "What if that monster never leaves the clock? You saw what happened in the library. The dark magic is spreading through the paintings now—infecting everything it touches!"

The Minotaur roared again—this time from farther away, Oliver thought—and Fennish turned his one eye on Meridian. "Please, old friend, just for a moment."

Meridian sighed wearily and, sitting down, proceeded to clean herself by licking her paw and brushing it behind her ear. Oliver sat down beside Algernon, who was moving Kenny's arms and legs as if fighting off some invisible foes.

"Samurais are cool," Oliver said after an awkward silence, but Algernon didn't respond, and went on throwing punches and kicks for Kenny. "Er—that wood glue of yours is cool, too. How'd you get to be such a good chemist?"

Algernon swung his head, flinging his bangs aside to reveal a wary green eye, then he set down Kenny and his jar of wood glue and fished out a necklace from under his shirt. At the end of the necklace was a locket. Algernon opened it. Inside was a picture of a Japanese man and a fair-haired woman—a woman who looked a lot like the painting of Abigail Blackford.

"Your parents?" Oliver asked. Algernon nodded, and pointed back and forth between his mother and the jar. "You mean, your mother taught you how to make the wood glue?"

Algernon made a "sort-of" gesture with his hand, then pointed back and forth between himself and the picture of his mother.

"Oh, of course. I'm an idiot. You mean your mother was a chemist like you."

Algernon smiled and nodded.

"Cool," Oliver said. "My mother was a ballet dancer. Before she met Pop, I mean. She also taught for a while at this school. But then she got sick and . . . well, she died two years ago."

Algernon pointed to his parents, then back and forth between himself and Oliver, and finally held up two fingers. Oliver understood that this meant Algernon's parents died two years ago, too.

"I'm sorry," Oliver said quietly. "And for, you know . . . everything."

Oliver wasn't sure what he meant by "everything"— Algernon losing his parents, the twins having to move here,

Ms. Graves—but all at once a lump lodged in his throat.

Algernon pointed at his mother, circled his fist on his heart, and pointed at Oliver. *I'm sorry about your mother,* he was saying, Oliver could tell. Then Algernon pointed at the picture of his father and gestured at Oliver as if to say, *Where is* your *father?*

Oliver dropped his eyes and pushed up his glasses. He'd refused to allow himself to worry about Pop since this nightmare began; but sure enough, all at once the lump in his throat threatened to turn into tears. And it might have, too, had they all not heard a faint scratching coming from the other side of the walled-off doorway.

Fennish and Meridian sprang up onto all fours and cocked their ears. More scratching, followed by a muffled "Oh dear—*oink-oink!*"

Oliver's heart soared. It was the pig, Reginald Eight!

"Reginald!" Meridian shouted at the wall. "Reginald, it's me, Meridian!"

"Oh, thank goodness you're safe!" the pig cried from the other side. "But you must get out of here while you still can! The monster is hunting us—*oink-oink!*"

"Reginald, where are the others?" Fennish asked. "Are they still alive?"

"I couldn't tell—*oink!* But you must get out of here before the monster catches you, too!" Reginald oinked and said something else that Oliver couldn't understand. The pig was speaking very fast and trying to keep his voice down.

"Say that again," Meridian said. "What do you mean you couldn't tell?"

Reginald squealed nervously. "The monster is putting us in the clock—*oink!* Nessie. I saw what the monster did to her and the others. Run away now before the monster catches you, too—*oink-oink!*"

"What are you talking about?" Fennish asked.

"There's no time to explain—*oink-oink!* Run away while you still—"

"*ROOOOOOAAARR!*"

Everyone staggered back. The Minotaur was on the other side of the walled-off doorway, but it sounded to Oliver as if the monster were right there in the hallway. The floor shook as the monster stomped closer, its hoof-beats like a bass drum going *boom-boom-boom!* Reginald uttered a final cry for help, and then the pig's muffled squeals began fading away as the monster thundered off. Oliver's heart seized.

The Minotaur had captured Reginald!

Oliver and the animals rammed their shoulders against the wall of sunstone, grunting and groaning as they tried desperately to push it open. Meridian cried out one last time for her friend, and then in the next moment, the pig's squeals were choked off and the hoofbeats abruptly stopped. Everyone backed away from the wall.

Poor Reginald Eight was gone.

"We've got to do something!" Meridian cried, breathless. Algernon whipped his bangs out of his eyes and looked helplessly at Oliver, who just stood there frozen in fear and confusion.

The Minotaur was putting the animals in the clock? But what did that mean?

"There's nothing we can do for him now," Fennish said. He sniffed at the air, and then started off down the hallway. Bewildered, Meridian and Algernon automatically followed, but Oliver's feet were rooted to the spot.

"Fennish," he called, and the others stopped. "Reginald said the Minotaur was putting the animals in the clock. Do you think he means the face or the mechanical room?"

Fennish heaved a heavy sigh. "All I know is that Blackford House cannot help them any more than it can help us. Our only hope is to find another way to the clock before the dark magic takes over for good."

"But what about the Minotaur?" Meridian cried. "Even if we make it to the clock, what's to say the monster won't catch us, too?"

"That might not be a bad idea," Fennish said, his one eye twinkling in the torchlight, and everyone gaped at him in confusion. "Perhaps we can distract the monster, get him to chase us long enough for the lads to rescue the others. Then, perhaps, we can find Ms. Graves."

Oliver and Algernon glanced at each other and gulped.

"I don't like it," Meridian said, shaking her head. "It's too dangerous."

"Better than bumbling around like fools in this maze," Fennish muttered.

And with that, the rat scurried off down the hallway with the others close behind. No one spoke, but Oliver's mind was a sea of questions. What did Reginald mean when he said the Minotaur was putting the animals in the clock? And were the animals still alive? Reginald said he couldn't tell!

Oliver breathed deeply and told himself to keep it together. The walls moving past him looked like those in the butler's hallway—which, when things were normal, was located beneath the clock—but Oliver wasn't sure that meant they were heading in the right direction. Oliver didn't know *what* to think anymore—especially a few moments later when the hallway dead-ended at a door.

"That's the door to the broom closet," Meridian said. "But what's it doing here?"

Fennish motioned with his paw for the others to stay put and cautiously approached the closet. A tense silence hung in the air as the rat sniffed around the bottom of the door, then pressed his ear against the wood and listened.

"I smell smoke," Fennish said. "And something else. Something . . . *musty.*"

"Musty?" Oliver said—but before Fennish could respond, a dull thud, followed by a panicky voice, came from behind the door.

"Oh, clumsy me!" someone uttered inside the closet. Everyone exchanged uneasy glances, and Fennish nodded at Oliver.

Oliver swallowed hard and, pushing up his glasses, slowly opened the door.

The inside of the broom closet was a mess, and there was a large, gaping hole in the back wall. Pieces of splintered wood and chunks of plaster were strewn everywhere. And there in the middle of it all, wobbling upside down at Oliver's feet, was a turtle shell.

# TEN

# THE WIRE

Lucy choked back a sob and hung her head. Her wrists throbbed from pounding on the wall, and her throat was sore from screaming. There was no sign of Agatha anywhere. And not only that, the hallway had been walled off at either end with sunstone. Lucy and Torsten were completely trapped!

"What are we going to do now?" the little dog cried.

Lucy hitched in a breath and, moving to one of the hallway walls, began searching for a secret passageway in the paneling. Torsten understood and began sniffing frantically along the baseboard. Lucy couldn't imagine how the little dog could smell anything except the smoldering remains of the chairs.

*Crack!*

Lucy whirled. Even from where she was standing, about thirty yards from the wall that had sealed off the dining room, Lucy could see that the sunstone bricks were beginning to change into blocks for the labyrinth. Torsten whimpered.

"It's those shadow wood branches from the painting," he said. "The dark magic infects everything it touches— just like those chairs!"

Lucy's eyes traveled up the chandelier's sagging chain and into the hole in the ceiling. She could make out the flicker of firelight up there, and there were broken slats of hardwood floor amid the shredded ceiling plaster. It had to be another room. Maybe even a way out!

"Stand back," Lucy said, gently pushing Torsten aside, and she unhooked the chain from the chandelier. Lucy quickly disconnected the wire and dragged the chandelier out of the way. It was still warm from the fire. Lucy wrapped the end of the chain around Torsten's belly.

"What are you doing?" Torsten asked, bewildered, as Lucy secured the chain with the hook from the chandelier. There was just enough slack for the chain to fit snugly under Torsten's front legs but still allow him to keep his paws on the floor.

"I'm going to climb up and then pull you up after me," Lucy said.

Torsten gulped audibly and began to tremble, but Lucy couldn't see what else to do. The wall was changing fast. Blackford House wouldn't be able to protect them for much longer.

Lucy patted Torsten on the head, and in the next moment, she was shinnying up the chain. She reached the floor above in a matter of seconds and poked her head up through the hole. Her heart began to hammer excitedly. She was in the parlor—and the light she had seen was coming from a roaring fire in the hearth.

But that wasn't the *only* thing in the hearth, Lucy knew. Before the labyrinth erupted, there had been an entrance to a secret underground passageway that led to the river. Lucy had used it on the night they rescued the animals from the Garr. If the passageway was still there, then maybe, just maybe . . .

Lucy pulled herself up a bit higher and climbed off the chain onto the floor. Her heart sank. The entire parlor had been destroyed in a massive fire, its furniture and countless antiques twisted black or gone altogether. What little remained looked almost alive in the flickering shadows, and where her family's portrait had hung above the hearth, there was now only a large black stain.

Lucy's eyes traveled up the chain again to yet *another* hole in the parlor ceiling. But there was not another floor up there, Lucy could tell, only a narrow shaft of shredded laths, into which the chain kept going and dissolved into the darkness.

That's where all the smoke went, Lucy thought. Could that scary shaft be like a chimney? What if it led to the roof?

Lucy shivered and looked around. Where the parlor windows and doorways had been, there were now the entrances to four more torch-lit hallways.

"Miss Lucy, hurry!" Torsten called up from the floor

below. "That wall is going to open at any moment!"

Lucy quickly pulled Torsten up to her level and unhooked him from the chain. The little dog groaned when he saw what had become of the parlor.

"But *why*?" he cried. Lucy ignored him. She felt almost dizzy now with desperation—if the labyrinth didn't destroy Blackford House, then the fire surely would!

Lucy quickly stomped on the three darkest stones in the hearth floor—this was how Fennish taught her to access the secret passageway—but instead of the stone door swinging open in the fireplace, the flames there whooshed out at her!

Lucy jumped back and threw up her hands. For a split second, she felt the heat singe the fuzz on her forearms, and then just as quickly, the flames shrank back into the hearth and the fire went on burning as before.

"Miss Lucy, are you all right?" Torsten cried, rushing up to her. Lucy patted herself all over to make sure she wasn't on fire, then shouted at the house:

*"WHAT IS WRONG WITH YOU?"*

Lucy's voice came back to her in broken echoes, and then she heard the distant rumble of a wall opening in the hallway below. Lucy moaned—it was the wall to the dining room, she knew. It had become part of the labyrinth.

Torsten whined and hurried over to the hallway where the foyer should have been.

"We need to get out of here before the dark magic reaches us!" he cried.

Lucy gazed up again at the darkened shaft. Even if she made it to the roof, she'd have to leave Torsten down here before she could pull him up. That was risky, especially now that the dark magic would be spreading down the hallway beneath them. What if the shadow wood branches found their way up here into the parlor? What if more furniture came to life?

Lucy felt on the verge of panic. She swallowed back a scream and gazed up again at the shaft. The shredded laths looked like rows of jagged teeth—never mind, who could tell what might be waiting for her up there in the darkness.

"But still," Lucy muttered to herself. "That smoke had to go somewhere."

Torsten read her mind and began backing away. "Oh no," he said. "You're not dragging me up there. That hole looks scarier than the Shadow Woods!"

"But, Torsten, what if that shaft is like a chimney and it leads us up onto the roof or something? We just can't keep trying these stupid hallways. We'll never get to the—"

Lucy stopped herself before *clock*, and her eyes swiveled back to the chandelier chain. The chandelier ran on electricity, which was generated by the clock. And everyone knew that electricity had to travel through—

"A wire!" Lucy blurted. She dashed over to the chain and, pulling it toward her, cried out with joy. The wire, woven through the links, ran all the way up into the shaft!

Lucy began to speak very fast. "Torsten—we need to see if this wire leads back to the clock. The wires are like veins coming from the house's heart!"

Torsten's jaw dropped. "You're out of your mind," he said. "That chain looks like it goes on forever. You'll never reach the top! I say we try another one of these hallways up here."

Out of the corner of her eye, Lucy noticed the hole in the parlor floor suddenly grow dimmer. The dark magic was spreading, snuffing out the torches in the hallway below as it had earlier in the hallway leading from the library!

"Torsten, please!" Lucy cried. "Blackford House is telling us what to do! This wire *must* lead to the clock. Look what's happening down there." Lucy pointed to the darkening hole in the floor, and Torsten's eyes bulged with fear. "We can't just keep walking blind through these hallways. This might be our only chance!"

The little dog hemmed and hawed a bit more. "All right," he said finally. "But I'm not waiting down here again! You go up in that hole, I'm going with you!"

Lucy pressed her lips together tightly. How could she climb the chain *and* carry Torsten at the same time? But then, gazing down at him, she got an idea: Algernon's bow tie bandage. Torsten was still wearing it.

Lucy quickly untied the bow tie from Torsten's neck and knotted it through a belt loop on the back of her shorts.

"You think you can hold on to this with your teeth while I climb?" she asked, jiggling the tie, and Torsten wagged his tail excitedly.

"Of course!" he exclaimed. "I *am* a *dog*, after all. And everyone knows that dogs have a first-rate pair of choppers!"

Torsten gnashed his teeth and smiled with his tongue lolling. Lucy smiled back and pulled the chain closer. Torsten stood on his hind legs, bit down on the bow tie, and in the next moment, Lucy began climbing up the chain with the little dog hanging from her waist. Torsten was heavier than she expected, and by the time she reached the ceiling, her arms and back muscles were aching.

As Lucy glanced down, the light coming from the hole in the parlor floor directly beneath her blinked out. The dark magic had taken over, snuffing out the torches in the hallway two floors below. Lucy moaned. Her arms and back felt as if they were on fire—but if she fell now, she would drop at least twenty feet into a sea of shadow wood branches. Or maybe something worse.

"*I mehwoo oywoo!*" Torsten said, his words garbled from the bow tie in his teeth.

"What?" Lucy cried, breathless. "Slow down so I can understand you!"

"*OY-WOO! I—meh-woo—OY-WOO!*" Torsten said deliberately, and somehow, Lucy understood him.

"Oil?" she asked. "You smell oil?"

Torsten began squirming excitedly at the end of the bow tie, sending a bolt of searing pain through Lucy's back. And yet she felt energized—the oil smell meant they were near the clock!

In a burst of strength, Lucy continued her ascent into the darkened shaft. A few more feet, and her hand struck the wire. It branched off from the chain and extended into what felt like a large hole in the laths. It was hard to tell for sure. Everything was so dark.

"*Dee oy-wooz in dere!*" Torsten cried, and without warning, he swung himself toward the wall, let go of the bow tie, and somehow scrambled up into the hole. "There's another shaft, Miss Lucy, big enough for you, too!"

Careful to avoid the wire, Lucy tried to do what Torsten had done. She swung herself closer to the wall and grabbed the lip of the shaft, squeezing the toes of her sneakers between the laths. The thin wooden slats buckled and split beneath her feet, but Lucy managed to climb up into the shaft before they broke apart altogether.

Lucy lay on her stomach, heart pounding and breathless in the dark. Her arms and back were throbbing, and she could barely move her fingers. This new, horizontal shaft was the same size as the vertical one—about three feet in diameter, Lucy estimated—but instead of laths lining the insides of it, the walls were made of smooth stone.

"You were right, Miss Lucy!" Torsten cried from up ahead of her. "There's loads of wires in here. And the smell of oil is stronger than ever!"

Lucy propped herself up onto her forearms and began moving forward—half crawling, half squirming through the narrow space like a worm in the dirt. A few seconds later, she caught sight of Torsten's faint, flickering shape about ten yards ahead. The little dog had stopped, and something was illuminating him from underneath. His tail wagged furiously as he motioned for Lucy to hurry.

Lucy moved faster, and in a matter of seconds joined Torsten at the edge of a large iron grate that had dozens of wires coming from its holes. The dim light spilling upward cast dancing, checkered shadows on the little dog's face. He raised his paw to his mouth—"*Ssh*"—and Lucy saw that the wires branched off into the mouths of three more darkened shafts.

Lucy crawled forward on her elbows and peered down through the grate. In the orangey light below, she could see a cluster of pipes directly beneath her. Lucy's heart nearly stopped.

It was the mechanical room!

Squealing with excitement, Lucy grabbed hold of the grate and, using all her might, slid it off to one side. The metal made a dull scraping sound that echoed through the shaft. Lucy froze and Torsten pricked his ears, the two of them ready to retreat if the Minotaur heard them. But the coast seemed clear. Lucy spread apart some wires that were in the way, wiggled herself around so that her legs draped over the opening, and then dropped feetfirst onto the pipes below.

The first thing Lucy noticed in the mechanical room was Tempus Crow in his place atop the cuckoo mechanism. Lucy gasped when she saw that the big black bird was wooden again. Then she noticed another thing: the other animals were nowhere to be found. Lucy's heart sank.

"Um, *helloooo*, did you forget something?" Torsten whispered.

The little dog leaped into Lucy's arms, and she climbed down with him the rest of the way to the floor.

"Where is everyone?" Torsten asked. "Do you think they escaped?"

Lucy shrugged and looked around. The mechanical room was a mess. There was a big puddle of oil near the rear of the clock face and her father's tools were scattered everywhere. But the clock's machinery appeared to be intact, including the switch for the fail-safe—which, much to Lucy's surprise, was in the *off* position.

"So, Ms. Graves *didn't* throw the fail-safe?" she wondered out loud.

"Tempus!" Torsten cried, gazing up at the crow. "You've gone wooden!"

Lucy's head was spinning. If Ms. Graves didn't throw the fail-safe, then how did she open the secret chamber? And if the clock was stopped, then why was Tempus Crow wooden?

"Let's get him down," Lucy said, but before she could set up her father's stepladder, the floor began to rumble with the *boom-boom-boom* of the Minotaur's hoofbeats—and they were getting closer!

"Quick!" Lucy cried, heading for the pipes. "Back up into the shaft!"

But then someone cried for help outside.

Lucy rushed out onto the landing and peered down over the railing. She was in a cavernous, dark-paneled chamber with torches everywhere. And there was the Minotaur below, roaring and dragging Agatha by her ankle up the stairs.

*"HELLLP!"* she cried, kicking and squirming.

Without thinking, Lucy dashed into the mechanical room, snatched up a large monkey wrench, and then ran back out again onto the landing. The Minotaur was on the landing now, too, struggling with Agatha at the top of the stairs—the monster's back was to Lucy, so it didn't see her right away.

Lucy rushed for the horned beast with the monkey wrench held high above her head. But before she could strike, Lucy saw something that stopped her in her tracks.

Dangling from the Minotaur's neck, nearly hidden in the folds of flesh beneath its massive jaws, was a large ruby pendant.

Lucy gasped. "Ms. Graves!"

"Lucy, no!" someone cried.

And then the monster was upon her.

# ELEVEN

# THE FEVER AND
# FREDERICK FIVE

"Frederick!" Oliver cried. He rushed into the closet and picked up the shell. "You can come out, Frederick! It's me, Oliver!"

The turtle's head and legs sprang from his shell as if on springs. "Oh, thank goodness, it's you!" he cried. "I thought you were the monster! And Fennish and Meridian—you're safe!"

"What happened, old friend?" Fennish asked, slipping with Meridian into the closet. Frederick craned his neck toward the hole in the wall.

"Oh, it was horrible!" he said, and Oliver felt the turtle tremble in his hands. "I'd somehow wandered into the kitchen, when I heard this awful racket coming from the hallway. I thought it might be the monster, but before I could find a place to hide, that new girl picked me up."

"Agatha!" Oliver cried, and Algernon squeezed into the closet with Kenny.

"Agatha, that's her name," the turtle said. "If not for Agatha, I'd be a goner. She saved me from the monster!"

"Where is she?" Meridian asked, her eyes swiveling back and forth between Frederick and the massive hole in the wall. Oliver could feel heat coming from the room beyond, but he couldn't see much. The room itself was dark, its jumbled contents black and twisted against the flickering orangey entrances of more torch-lit hallways. And the smell of smoke was almost nauseating.

"Horrible, horrible, I tell you!" Frederick said, retreating a bit into his shell. "One moment I was there on the floor, and the next, Agatha picked me up and I saw Lucy running toward us with Torsten. They were being chased down the hallway by a horde of dining room chairs!"

Everyone gasped. "The dark magic," Meridian said. "It infects everything it touches!"

"But Blackford House saved them!" Frederick said, sticking out his head again. "The chandelier from the foyer crashed through the ceiling and squashed the chairs to bits! And what chairs it didn't squash, the fire took care of *them*. One of the torches—it spewed out flames and burned them up on the spot! Just like the table and chairs there in the kitchen!"

"You mean—*that's* the kitchen?" Meridian asked, nodding at the hole, and Oliver moaned. This couldn't be possible!

"Everything happened so fast," Frederick said. "After Agatha picked me up, I heard something moving behind us there in the kitchen—'*Not again!*' I heard her say—and then a stone wall blocked us off from Lucy and Torsten!"

"The house was protecting you!" Meridian cried.

"Right, but it wasn't done yet. Next thing I know, the

chairs in the kitchen were coming after us, too. They were monsters, I tell you—just like the ones in the hallway. Agatha hid us here in the closet, and then—*whoosh!*—we heard the entire kitchen go up in flames. It was horrible! The flames lapped at us from underneath the door, and then . . . well, I can't explain it, but the broom closet spun around, turning us away from the fire!"

Fennish's one eye swiveled toward the kitchen. "Blackford House is trying to burn away the infection," he said. "The fire is its last defense!"

"But where is Agatha now?" Oliver cried. "And Lucy and Torsten?"

"I don't know what happened to the others after the wall separated us, but Agatha"—Frederick gulped—"that's where the hole came from. The fire was over as quickly as it began. The closet was dark, and Agatha knocked something over. I fear the monster must've heard her, because next thing I knew, it burst through the wall, snatched Agatha from the closet, and carried her away!"

Algernon began signing frantically. Oliver understood.

"We've got to find her!" he cried.

"Wait here a moment!" Fennish snapped, and he leaped through the hole into the kitchen. Oliver lost sight of him for a moment amid the darkened, twisted wreckage, and then the rat's dim shape appeared in the entrance to one of the hallways. He sniffed around a bit, and then Oliver lost him again in the darkness. Algernon made some more frantic hand gestures.

"Don't worry, lad," Meridian whispered, reaching out her paw. "Fennish is tracking the scent of the Minotaur. We'll find your sister, I promise."

Now Fennish was in the entrance to a different hallway, Oliver saw. The rat sniffed around there for a bit, too, then once again slipped back into the gloom. A few seconds later, Fennish was back. He perched himself on the edge of the hole and motioned with his muzzle for the others to follow.

"Did you pick up the scent?" Meridian asked, and Fennish nodded.

"Aye, and something else. But take care. Things are still hot."

Fennish hopped back down into the kitchen. Meridian jumped through the hole after him, followed by Algernon, and finally Oliver with Frederick tucked under his arm.

Oliver flicked on his watch light. The kitchen had been completely obliterated—everything that was burnable, gone. And what wasn't burnable—the refrigerator, the stove—was half-melted. Only the grand porcelain sink appeared unharmed. It stood murky and gray, like a ghost in the shadows.

"Poor Blackford House," Frederick said, poking his head out from his shell.

As Oliver drew closer to the hallway, his light fell on the twisted metal remains of the kitchen chairs—the same chairs in which they had all sat at breakfast that morning. They were in a pile, their legs rutted and black like the legs of some giant spider. Oliver's stomach knotted. Fennish was right. Blackford House *was* trying to burn away the infection, he thought—when his watch light accidentally caught something in the ceiling. Oliver stopped.

Where the kitchen's light fixture had once hung, there was now a gaping hole—Oliver could just make out the light fixture's chain running up into it from the floor. Maybe that's where the smoke went, he thought. Maybe the house even made the hole on purpose. . . .

"Oliver!" Meridian shouted, startling him from his thoughts. Oliver joined the others in the hallway and gasped. There was a trail of ashen hoofprints leading away from the kitchen. Oliver's heart began to hammer. There could be no doubt—the Minotaur had gone this way!

Oliver and the others followed the hoofprints around a corner and came to another walled-off doorway—this one made of blocks from the labyrinth. The hoofprints dead-ended in front of it.

"No!" Oliver groaned. Fennish sniffed around at the

base of the wall, and then slumped onto his hind legs and hung his head.

"It is useless," the rat said with a sigh. "Blackford House is losing its fight. It couldn't move this wall for us even if it wanted to."

Algernon hugged Kenny close, burying his face in the samurai's tangled hair, and then Meridian hissed.

"Look!" she cried, her back arching in fear. Oliver followed her gaze to a patch of darkness about thirty yards down the hallway. And the darkness was *coming closer*, spreading out across the ceiling and the floor and the walls in zigzagging, vein-like patterns that reminded Oliver of—

"Branches," he rasped, and then one of the torches farther down the hall sparked and sputtered before being snuffed out altogether by the creeping darkness.

"The dark magic!" Fennish cried, springing to his feet. "The infection is spreading this way!"

"We must turn back!" Meridian shouted, hurrying past Oliver.

But Oliver didn't follow, and instead ran straight toward the oncoming darkness.

"Lad, no!" Fennish cried, but Oliver just ignored him, and snatched one of the torches from the wall just before the darkness consumed it.

"Don't let the dark magic touch you!" Meridian shrieked.

Oliver raced back toward the others with the torch in hand. If only he could save more than just one! Fire was Blackford House's last defense against the dark magic, Fennish had said. If the fire went out, then Blackford House would die. Just like—

"Mom," Oliver blurted, stopping in his tracks. A thought had caught him by surprise, but the others didn't hear him. They were already heading back toward the kitchen.

"What are you waiting for?" Frederick cried—Oliver had forgotten the turtle was still tucked under his arm.

"Of course," Oliver said, his mind suddenly racing. "Soon after Mom started chemo, she got an infection and had this bad fever. The doctor said fever is the body's natural defense mechanism. The fire—it's like Blackford House has a fever, too. But most of the time fever isn't enough. The body needs help—you know, like medicine."

"*Medicine?*" Frederick asked, bewildered.

"That's right," Oliver said, moving to the wall of labyrinth blocks. "So, let's be the medicine."

Oliver pushed up his glasses, and with a deep breath, touched the torch to the stone. The wall flashed brightly, then burst into bluish-white flames that rippled outward from the point of contact. Oliver recoiled as the flames rippled faster, and then in the middle of the stones appeared a hole. The hole quickly grew larger until the flames dissolved into the entrance to another torch-lit hallway—a hallway with a trail of ashen hoofprints fading off into the gloom up ahead.

"You did it!" Frederick cried, and then he called to the others. "Fennish, Meridian, Oliver did it!"

The animals hurried back, their mouths hanging open in shock, but there was no time to ask how Oliver opened the wall.

"*HELLLP!*" someone screamed from farther down this newest hallway.

"*ROOOOOOAAARR!*"

"Agatha!" Oliver cried, rushing forward with the torch in hand. The others were close behind, the screaming and roaring growing louder with every step. Oliver followed the hoofprints around a bend, and then the hallway opened into a cavernous, torch-lit version of the foyer.

Oliver could hardly believe his eyes. There was Blackford House's grand, richly paneled staircase stretching up in front of him to the clock. Agatha was at the top of the stairs, hanging on to the railing for dear life as the Minotaur tried dragging her by her ankles onto the landing. And there was Lucy on the landing, too. She was running toward the monster with a monkey wrench poised above her head to strike. Then, for some reason, Lucy stopped cold and cried:

"Ms. Graves!"

"Lucy, no!" Oliver screamed.

But he was too late. The Minotaur had seen her, and with a swipe of its massive claws, the monster knocked Lucy backward into the clock.

# TWELVE

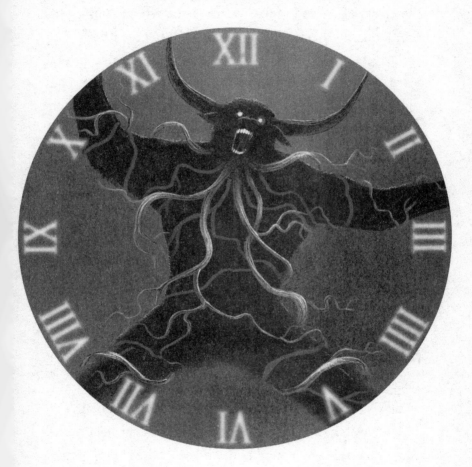

# THE TRUTH ABOUT
# KENZO

At first, Lucy felt only the dull thud of her body against the clock. She was vaguely aware of the wrench falling to the floor, and then she realized she couldn't breathe.

Lucy teetered dizzily on her heels and, stumbling forward, grabbed hold of the railing to keep from falling. The monster had knocked the wind out of her. The backs of her eyes felt fuzzy and her ears were ringing.

*"ROOOOOOAAARR!"*

Lucy shook her head, and bolts of bright white pain flared across her eyes. Agatha was screaming again—and now Oliver, too.

*"HEY, BULL-FACE, OVER HERE!"* he cried. Oliver was holding a torch and running up the stairs with Meridian and Fennish close behind. Algernon was there, too, clutching Kenny and his jar of wood glue. And was that Frederick Five at the bottom of the stairs? It was too dark there to tell for sure, and then Lucy's eyes fell on Oliver again as he raised his torch to attack the Minotaur.

*Oliver, no!* Lucy tried to scream—but she had no air.

Lucy watched in silent terror as the monster held on to Agatha's ankle with one hand, and with the other, batted the torch from Oliver's grasp.

*"ROOOOOOAAARR!"*

Oliver and the animals backed away down the

stairs—when out of nowhere, Torsten flew past Lucy and leaped onto the Minotaur's back.

Everything happened so fast that Lucy didn't have time to react. Torsten seized the monster's neck in his jaws, upon which the Minotaur let go of Agatha, tore the little dog free, and shoved him into his *six* hole.

"Torsten!" Lucy cried, finally able to breathe, but she was too late. Torsten was wooden now—just like all the other animals!

*"NO!"* Lucy cried out in horror, but it was true. The animals were wooden again and in their holes, she registered in one moment, and in the next, the Minotaur was coming for her again, its arms open wide as if to hug her.

Lucy ducked out of the way just in time and ran into Oliver and Algernon by the stairs. Oliver pulled her back, and as the Minotaur whirled on them, Algernon hurled his jar of wood glue at the monster, hitting it square between the eyes. The glass shattered, and the monster howled, throwing its hands up to its face as a mask of thick, grayish goop ran down to its neck.

And then something very strange happened.

Algernon's wood glue began to pop and sparkle. Lucy barely had time to blink when, without warning, dozens of shadow wood branches exploded out from underneath the Minotaur's muzzle. The creature roared and tried to pull them free, but the branches quickly fanned out all over the Minotaur's hairy body and fixed themselves to the clock, pushing the monster backward and pinning it there like a giant spider holding its prey.

Lucy gaped in amazement as the monster roared and struggled against the tangle of branches, and then just as quickly, the branches began to wither and break.

"Meridian, look!" Fennish cried. "The stone!"

The shadow wood branches had shriveled back so that the ruby pendant was now visible beneath the Minotaur's snarling maw. And before Lucy realized what was happening, Meridian scrambled up onto the tangle of branches and tore the pendant from the monster's neck.

The Minotaur howled, the branches crumbled all around, and then the monster and Meridian fell together to the floor in a heap of billowing ashes. Meridian scrambled away as the ashes dissolved into a blanket of purple sparkles that covered the Minotaur entirely. The sparkles began to flash, and with each flash, the Minotaur got smaller and smaller until the flashing stopped and there sat Ms. Graves, good as new and blinking up at everyone half-dazed.

Agatha cried out for joy, Algernon dropped Kenny, and the twins rushed forward to hug Ms. Graves. Agatha asked her what had happened, but the governess could only gaze back at everyone in confusion.

"I'm sorry" was all she could say. Meridian spat out the pendant on the floor.

"This is the cause of all our troubles," the cat said.

"Aye," Fennish said, sniffing at the pendant. "We've seen its like before."

"But not in ages," Frederick Five chimed in; because he was a turtle, it had taken him the longest to reach the landing. As Lucy scooped Frederick up in her arms and kissed him, Agatha picked up the pendant and rose to her feet.

"Look at this," she said. Lucy and Oliver gathered around, and in the dim light, Lucy saw the engraving of a bull head on the back of the ruby's gold setting.

"It's a Minotaur," Lucy said. "Fennish, where have you seen this jewel before?"

The animals regarded one another anxiously.

"The Blackfords used a similar amulet in their alchemy," Fennish said.

"An amulet?" Oliver asked.

"Aye. But Mrs. Blackford always referred to it as a philosopher's stone."

"A philosopher's stone?" Agatha asked. "You mean, like the one alchemists supposedly use to transform lead into gold?"

"It seems the stone can transform all sorts of things," Meridian said. "You saw for yourself what it can do. The amulet reacted strangely with the wood glue. It transformed it into a web of branches."

"Aye," Fennish said, his one eye twinkling in the torchlight. "And that's not the only thing the amulet transformed." Fennish nodded at Ms. Graves.

"That was the flash of red light Lucy saw in the clock," Oliver said. "The amulet transformed Ms. Graves into the Minotaur!"

"And Blackford House into a labyrinth," Agatha said. "The philosopher's stone must have reacted to something in the clock the same way it reacted to the wood glue."

"The conductor sphere," Oliver said. "That's what mixes the magic from the clock animals and pumps it to the rest of the house. The same thing must have happened with the amulet's dark magic. That's what started the spread of the infection!"

Agatha pointed to the bull head on the back of the stone's setting. "I'll bet you this engraving has something to do with it. Perhaps the amulet is cursed."

"But Mr. Snockett gave me that amulet," said Ms. Graves. "He told me never to take it off. In fact, I felt I *couldn't* take it off—as if I were hypnotized."

Lucy gasped. "But then that would mean Mr. Snockett is—"

"An alchemist," Oliver said, finishing her sentence, and Agatha scoffed.

"Uncle Oscar an alchemist? That's absurd!"

"But he gave Ms. Graves the amulet," Lucy said.

"But why would he want to turn Ms. Graves into a Minotaur?" Agatha asked.

"And why would you put our friends back in the clock?" Meridian asked, moving closer to Ms. Graves. "What did you do to them? When the clock is stopped, they should be alive!"

Ms. Graves just blinked back at Meridian with eyes full of tears.

"The dark magic," Fennish said, gazing up at the clock. "When it all began, the pendulum stopped just long enough for us to escape before the clock became infected. After that, the clock became part of the labyrinth. Look."

Fennish jerked his muzzle at the clock and everyone gasped. Upon closer inspection, Lucy discovered that the once white-painted sunstone bricks had transformed into blocks for the labyrinth.

"It can't be," Meridian said in shock, and Fennish heaved a raspy sigh.

"I'm afraid the others are infected now, too," he said sadly. "The clock animals are part of the labyrinth."

"No!" Lucy shouted, rushing for Torsten. She tried to pull him out of his *six* hole, but the little dog statue wouldn't budge. "Please, help me!" Lucy cried, turning back to the others, but before anyone could react, Agatha squealed in pain.

"He bit me!" she cried, shaking out her hand, and then Lucy spied Kenny scrambling up the clock face with the amulet dangling from his tiny hand. Lucy's eyes bulged, and her mouth hung open. She couldn't believe what she was seeing.

Somehow, the little samurai had come to life! And he had stolen the amulet!

"Stop him!" Oliver cried, and without thinking, Meridian bounded up the clock face after Kenny.

"Meridian, no!" Fennish screamed, and in the blink of an eye, the cat was sucked into her *twelve* hole and turned wooden again. Lucy cried out in horror, and then Kenny disappeared through the cuckoo door.

Lucy and Oliver rushed into the mechanical room—Kenny was up on the cuckoo mechanism now beside Tempus Crow.

"Not so fast, you little brats," Kenny said in a husky voice, and he aimed the amulet at the children. The red jewel swelled with light like a burning coal. "One false move and I'll show you more of what this stone can do!"

Lucy, bewildered, sensed the others gathering in the doorway behind her.

"So glad you could join us, Ms. Graves," Kenny said. "My plan had been to kill you once you'd stopped the clock, but I now realize that my dear niece is right. This amulet *is* cursed. Sorry for the inconvenience—but then again, I *am* paying you quite handsomely!"

Kenny howled with laughter, and Ms. Graves gasped.

"Mr. Snockett?" she cried, and the little samurai bowed dramatically.

"At your service," he said. "And I do hope you'll forgive me for turning you into a Minotaur. But you see, only a monster with superhuman strength could both stop the clock and not damage the conductor sphere. Then, while Blackford House was preoccupied with evicting you, I would've been able to execute the next phase of my plan. I never expected the amulet would transform Blackford House into a labyrinth, but once again my dear niece is right: the amulet reacted strangely with the magic here— which means the conductor sphere is even more powerful than I imagined!"

Lucy's head was spinning—so much was coming at her at once. Kenny was Oscar Snockett? But how? And why was he talking about the conductor sphere? Lucy opened her mouth to ask, but then Fennish scurried into the mechanical room and hopped up onto one of the pipes, ready to attack. The little samurai leveled the amulet at him, and Lucy quickly snatched the rat up into her arms.

"Fennish, no!" she cried. "He'll kill you!"

"Oh, no I won't," said Mr. Snockett. "He and the turtle must join our little party there in the clock!"

The puppet laughed, and Lucy thought for a moment that she might go insane. Having to be around Samurai Kenny when he was just a puppet was bad enough, but now seeing the life in his eyes and watching his lips moving with the voice of an old man . . . well, it was almost too much for Lucy's mind to handle.

"But—you *can't* be Uncle Oscar—" Agatha stammered. "You're still in England!"

The little samurai sneered. "You fool. It was I, your dear uncle Oscar, who gave Kenzo to your father shortly before he died. That was the *first* part of my plan. For you see, Kenzo is really a centuries-old Japanese doll capable of housing an alchemist's shadow—which is how my spirit traveled with you all the way from England while my body remained behind!"

Mr. Snockett laughed. Agatha just stared back at him, dumbstruck, and Lucy felt Ms. Graves tense behind her.

"Don't you see?" Mr. Snockett went on. "I needed a way to get to the conductor sphere without Blackford House evicting me. Kenzo was my only hope; for the very magic that holds my shadow inside also blocks Blackford House from sensing my intentions. I'd been biding my time ever since we arrived, waiting for Ms. Graves to enter the clock so I could activate the amulet and transform her into the Minotaur. But then the labyrinth got in my way and I had to bide my time again."

"Of course," Oliver cried. "That's why you suddenly showed up in the foyer when the house was changing. You were near the clock when it happened!"

Mr. Snockett smiled. "Fortunately, the house was so distracted with everything else, it didn't realize that I was the real culprit. A happy accident of which I took full advantage. Until now."

Oliver impulsively stepped forward, and Mr. Snockett leveled the amulet at him.

"Don't do anything foolish, lad. But you can make yourself useful by giving me that wrench there at your feet." Oliver hesitated, and Mr. Snockett thrust the amulet at him. The red jewel's glow intensified. "Give it to me now, or I'll take it the hard way!"

"Do as he says, lad," Fennish whispered from Lucy's arms, and Oliver reluctantly picked up the wrench and handed it to Mr. Snockett. Lucy thought it looked almost comical in the samurai's tiny hands.

Keeping the amulet aimed at Oliver, Mr. Snockett touched the wrench to the conductor sphere and— *ZAAAAAAP!*—tendrils of electricity shot out at the doll's hand. The wrench went flying, and Mr. Snockett growled in frustration.

"Blackford House may be weak," Fennish said, "but it knows what you're up to now. It will never let you take its conductor sphere!"

Mr. Snockett exhaled wearily. "For the time being. But that will change once you and that turtle are back in the clock. You were right, my one-eyed friend. The clock is now part of the labyrinth, which means you animals will soon be part of it, too."

"I remember now," muttered Ms. Graves. "When I was the monster, my only desire was to return the animals to the clock—as if I knew it would help the labyrinth!"

"Indeed," said Mr. Snockett. "After all, a bull's basic instinct is to defend its territory. That's what the Minotaur was doing, I suspect. Defending its territory and fortifying its lair. The clock animals have always been Blackford House's biggest threat, its secret weapon. But once all of them become part of the labyrinth—"

"Blackford House will die," Lucy muttered, her heart aching.

"One more blast from this amulet should do the trick," said Mr. Snockett, admiring it. "The magic from the cursed philosopher's stone will combine with the magic in the conductor sphere, travel through the pipes, and then be circulated through the rest of the house, thus completing the labyrinth. Same concept as before, only this time, I shall get things going *on purpose*."

"Then you can get whatever's inside the conductor sphere," Agatha said. "That's what you're really after, isn't it, Uncle? What's *inside*?"

"Precisely," Mr. Snockett said with a satisfied sigh. "If only you knew how long I've waited for this moment. But after old Mortimer double-crossed me, I wasn't quite sure it would happen."

Lucy gasped. "Mortimer—you mean, Mortimer Quigley?"

"Not long after I became guardian to the twins, I sent old Mortimer to Watch Hollow to get me the conductor sphere. A delicate operation given Blackford House's defenses. But the bumbling old fool betrayed me and tried to use the magic here for himself"—Mr. Snockett admired his tiny doll hands—"which is why *this* time I took matters into my own hands. Just like on the night Hiroto Kojima crashed his car."

Lucy's heart skipped a beat and she turned to the others. Ms. Graves's and the twins' faces were frozen in shock.

"You see, once I learned the truth about Blackford House, a house I had no chance of inheriting, I needed *someone else* to inherit it for me." Mr. Snockett narrowed his eyes hatefully at the twins. "My shadow was in Kenzo that night in the car. *I* killed your parents, you little brats— just as I am going to kill your friends now!"

The amulet swelled with light; and at the same time, Fennish leaped from Lucy's arms and tackled Mr. Snockett from the conductor sphere. The samurai doll shrieked in surprise, and then a blinding bolt of red light shot across the mechanical room. Everyone jumped back onto the landing as the blast ricocheted off the walls and exploded against the pipes, and in the next moment, Lucy saw Fennish scurrying for the door.

"*RUN!*" the rat cried. Agatha grabbed Lucy by the arm, and the two of them sprinted across the landing to the stairs.

"*YOU'RE TOO LATE!*" Mr. Snockett cried from the clock. The old man howled with laughter, but it was quickly drowned out by the deafening creaks and groans coming from the walls all around.

Then, without warning, the stairs collapsed beneath

Lucy's feet. She fell onto her backside and began sliding down a ramp with the others, faster and faster as the incline steepened. Everyone screamed—but not Lucy. Her eyes were fixed on a rapidly narrowing strip of sunlight high above her head—so high that Lucy was sure it would be the last thing she'd ever see.

# THIRTEEN

## CLAM CAKES

Oliver sat up and looked around. The ramp had deposited him in a narrow, shadowy passage. There was light coming from somewhere, but there were no torches, and the walls stretched off into the gloom on either side of him as far as he could see.

Oliver staggered to his feet and trained his eyes upward, higher and higher, until they settled on a thin band of sunlight way up at the top of the passage. Oliver's breath stuck in his throat and his heart began to hammer.

The walls had to be at least a hundred feet high!

"Where are we?" Lucy cried—she and the others were on their feet now, too. "Where are Fennish and Frederick?"

"The clock," Oliver said. "I saw them sucked up into their holes."

Lucy's eyes grew wide. *"What?"*

"When Snockett fired the amulet, it must have strengthened the clock's magnetic pull before traveling through the rest of the house. The animals are all infected now."

Lucy moaned in despair. "But that means—"

"The labyrinth is com-*plete*," Oliver said, his voice cracking with emotion, and then Agatha and Algernon started crying. Ms. Graves hugged the twins close. It was all too much for them to bear—Lucy, too, Oliver saw, and she turned away from him with eyes full of tears.

"It's our fault," Agatha sputtered between sobs. "Uncle Oscar killed Mother and Father so we would inherit Blackford House. After Mr. Quigley betrayed him, he used us to bring Kenzo here so he could steal whatever is in that conductor sphere. And you, Ms. Graves—Uncle turned you into a monster because of us"—Agatha looked around— "all of this is because of *us!*"

Ms. Graves pressed her lips together and inhaled sharply.

"No more of that," she said, stiffening her spine. "You mustn't even think such a thing. Oscar Snockett is the only one to blame, and I for one don't plan on letting him get away with it." Ms. Graves thumbed away the tears from under Algernon's bangs. "Now, the first thing we need to do is to find a way out of this labyrinth."

"But what about the animals?" Lucy cried. "We can't just leave them here!"

"Good heavens, young lady!" cried Ms. Graves. "You're not thinking about going back to the clock, are you?"

"Ms. Graves is right, Lucy," Oliver said. "Even if we could find our way back, how would we get the animals out? They're all infected, and the clock is messed up."

Algernon tugged on Agatha's sleeve to get her attention, then made some quick hand gestures. Agatha dragged her wrist across her eyes and began to translate as her brother kept signing.

"Not messed up, just stopped, Algy says. Even though the animals are infected, Algy noticed they hadn't changed to stone for the labyrinth. They were all still made of shadow wood and sunstone. Which means—" Agatha's eyes brightened with understanding. "Of course! Algy, you're a genius!"

Algernon shrugged as if to say, I know, but Oliver could only stand there like an idiot.

"Don't you see?" Agatha went on. "Uncle said it himself. The clock animals have always been Blackford House's secret weapon. They are resisting their transformation, fighting the infection just like the house was. Which means—"

"They're still alive *inside*!" Lucy cried.

"And whatever's inside that conductor sphere is still there, too," Agatha said. "Perhaps if we get the clock ticking and all the magic flowing properly again—well, there might still be enough time to set things right."

Algernon nodded excitedly, but Oliver only sighed and shook his head.

"But there's no way to get the clock ticking again. The fail-safe didn't work."

Lucy's eyes grew wide. "The fail-safe!" she cried, but Oliver just blinked back at her blankly. "Ollie, the fail-safe was in the *off* position. Ms. Graves never switched it on like we thought—did you, Ms. Graves?"

The governess thought for a moment, then shook her head.

"You see?" Lucy said. "That means the fail-safe might still work!"

Oliver opened his mouth to speak but then stopped himself. Pop had outfitted the fail-safe with a manual override connected to the old winding mechanism. If Algernon was right and the animals were still made of shadow wood and sunstone, the clock theoretically would start ticking again if he flipped the switch. And if the conductor sphere could pump some of the old magic back into the house— well, maybe the twins were right. Maybe things *would* go back to normal!

"We need to get to the clock before Snockett gets into that conductor sphere!" Oliver cried, his heart hammering with excitement.

"But how are we going to do that?" asked Ms. Graves, looking around. "The labyrinth is larger than ever!"

Before Oliver could reply, a voice called faintly from above:

*"Hey, kids, is that you?"*

"Pop!" Oliver cried—but the walls were so high, the angle so steep, that Oliver could barely make out the silhouette of his father's head against the narrow strip of sky.

"The front door was locked!" he shouted down to Oliver and the others. "I tried to find another way in, but then the house grew a hundred feet high and trapped me on top of this maze! What the heck is going on?"

"Pop!" Oliver called up to him. "Can you see the clock?"

Agatha squeezed Oliver's arm and smiled—she knew what he was thinking. Maybe Pop could lead them back to the clock. Oliver felt his cheeks go hot, and when he looked up again, his father was gone. A tense silence passed, and then the hazy shape of Mr. Tinker's head reappeared against the sky.

"Yes, I see it!" he called down to his son. "But never mind about that! We've got to get you guys out of there!"

"Pop, you need to help us get to the clock first!" Lucy shouted.

"The clock?" he cried in disbelief. "Are you out of your mind? I'm getting you out of there!"

"There's no time to explain, Charles!" Ms. Graves called up to him. "Just tell us how to reach the clock!"

Another tense silence passed, during which Oliver could sense his father struggling with what to do. He was just about to call up to him again when something dropped into the passage a few yards away. Oliver rushed over and picked it up.

It was a piece of clam cake.

"Follow my lead!" Mr. Tinker called down, and Oliver heard another piece drop in the gloom farther down the passageway. He raced toward it, and then everyone fell in behind him as they followed Mr. Tinker's trail of clam cakes through the labyrinth.

Unfortunately, after about ten minutes, Mr. Tinker could go no farther—his wall had dead-ended, he explained, and it was too dangerous for him to jump across to another. He briefly tried to shout down directions, but that proved impossible—the walls were too high, and he couldn't see the others when they turned the corner. And so, Mr. Tinker tossed down the remainder of the clam cakes. There was only one bag left.

"You're on your own now!" he cried. "Just leave yourself a trail so you don't cover the same ground twice!"

Mr. Tinker wished everyone luck, and Oliver and the others pressed on, leaving a trail of clam cake pieces behind them. It was slow going, and after another ten minutes of wrong turns and backtracking, they finally exited into a large, open-air courtyard.

In the middle of the courtyard was a hundred-foot-tall tower with a set of stone steps spiraling up around it to the clock at the top. The whole thing looked like a bizarre version of Big Ben, as if the mechanical room had been extracted from the house, placed in a box, and plopped down atop a twisted tree branch.

Ms. Graves took the lead then, and the children followed her up the stairs, round and round the tower, until they were about ten feet from the clock. Ms. Graves motioned for everyone to stop, and Oliver bent over, heart hammering and short of breath.

"Now what do we do?" Agatha whispered, panting, and Oliver crept closer to the clock. His heart squeezed—Algernon was right, the animals were still made of shadow wood and sunstone—but then Oliver noticed the mechanical room door was open a crack, and a low buzzing could be heard coming from within. A moment later, *clank!*

Oliver tiptoed to the door and peeked inside. Mr. Snockett's back was to him, but Oliver could see that the little samurai was trying to fish something out from the conductor sphere with his tiny hands. The amulet lay smoking on the floor nearby. Mr. Snockett had used the magical jewel to cut a hole in the conductor sphere!

Before he could think twice about the wisdom of it, Oliver burst into the mechanical room and snatched up the amulet from the floor.

Mr. Snockett whirled and fired what looked like a spindly magic wand at Oliver, hitting him with a bolt of bright white lightning in the chest. The amulet went flying and Oliver staggered back dizzily toward the door. At the same time, Ms. Graves entered the mechanical room and helped him keep his feet. Oliver shook his head, and the dizziness lifted. He was unharmed, it seemed; the lightning had only stunned him.

Mr. Snockett frowned at the magic wand. "Not meant to be used as a weapon," he muttered, and then Oliver became aware of Lucy and the twins gathering behind him. Mr. Snockett aimed the magic wand in their direction. "Take care, brats! I can still send you falling to your deaths from this tower!"

"Please, Mr. Snockett," said Ms. Graves, throwing herself in front of Oliver. "Don't hurt them!"

Mr. Snockett laughed and hopped up higher onto the pipes. "Hurt them?" he said, his bulging eyes wild with delight. "Oh, no, no, no! I shall not hurt them—at least not until the final part of my plan. For I have finally found what we alchemists have been in search of for centuries!"

"Immortality," Lucy said, slipping into the room, and Mr. Snockett swiveled his eyes at her. "Edgar Blackford told us that's why his parents built this clock. They wanted to make themselves immortal."

"Very good!" Mr. Snockett replied, brandishing the magic wand. "But with the help of this, I shall use the Shadow Woods to become something more powerful than any Blackford could've imagined. For you see, to become immortal, I will need a *human* body to house my shadow. And what better than a child's in which to embrace eternity?"

Oliver gasped, and his mouth hung open. He couldn't believe what he was hearing, and yet he understood just the same. Oscar Snockett had killed the Kojimas' parents not only so he could get to the conductor sphere, but also so he could possess either Agatha or Algernon. He wanted to use one of their bodies the same way he used Kenzo the puppet!

"But now I have *four* children's bodies from which to choose," said Mr. Snockett. "Which one of you will it be? Which one of you will help this old alchemist become immortal?"

"Never!" cried Ms. Graves, shielding Lucy and Oliver.

"Consider yourself fired, then," said Mr. Snockett with a wave of his hand—but nothing happened. The samurai's eyes flickered with alarm, and he waved his hand again.

"Looking for this?" Agatha said, entering the room, too, and she held up the amulet. Oliver's heart swelled. Agatha just never ceased to amaze him!

"Give that back to me," Mr. Snockett said. He waved his hand again, and Agatha's hand jerked forward, as if the amulet were trying to escape. Agatha clapped her other hand around it and clutched the amulet to her chest. Mr.

Snockett growled and leveled the wand at her, upon which Algernon jumped in front of his sister to protect her.

"Don't worry, he can't hurt you," Oliver said. "That wand isn't meant to be used as a weapon. You said so yourself, Snockett."

The little samurai's eyes darted frantically around the room. Oliver understood. Everyone was inside the clock now. There was no chance of them falling from the tower if he shot them with his wand. Oliver met Lucy's eyes. She understood, too.

"Go ahead, Snockett," she said, moving closer. "You can't shoot us all before we get to you."

"Not to mention, you're just as much a prisoner of this labyrinth as we are," added Ms. Graves.

"Am I?" he said with a sneer. "Do you think some silly maze can stop me?"

Mr. Snockett reached over and threw the fail-safe switch. Once again, nothing happened.

"Nice try," Oliver said. "But the clock won't work without the magic of the conductor sphere."

Mr. Snockett smiled mischievously. "Precisely," he said.

And with that, Mr. Snockett flicked the magic wand, shooting a continuous, pulsating beam of bright white light into the conductor sphere. Everyone staggered back, holding on to each other for support as the light quickly spread through the pipework. At the same time, Oliver became aware of gears clanking and springs boinging all around.

"Look out!" Lucy cried, and she pulled Oliver out of the way just in time to avoid the swinging pendulum.

"The clock is ticking again!" Agatha shouted, and then the whole mechanical room began to shake as if from an earthquake. Oliver hung on to some pipes for support—not only was the room shaking, he realized, it was falling, too!

Oliver screamed, but Mr. Snockett only laughed and continued to pump the pulsating beam of light into the conductor sphere.

"The magic wand!" Agatha cried, grabbing hold of Oliver's elbow. "Uncle is killing the infection—changing the house back to normal so he can escape!"

Despite his terror, Oliver somehow understood. Mr. Snockett was acting as the fail-safe. He was pumping the life-giving, sunstone-and-shadow-wood-mixing magic of the conductor sphere back into the house *himself*—and at a higher concentration than ever before!

But still, Oliver was so terrified he couldn't breathe. And then, in a final burst of blinding white light, the mechanical room landed with a heavy thud. Tools clanked and bounced everywhere, and Mr. Snockett turned off the beam from the magic wand. Oliver's eyes were full of floaters, but he could see that the pendulum had stopped again.

Mr. Snockett leaped up onto the pipes and into the port-hole, which was open and bright with afternoon sunlight. Oliver could also hear a low rumbling noise coming from outside. It shook the floor and rattled the tools—like when the busses used to drive by the clock shop in the city.

"Just as I suspected!" cried Mr. Snockett, turning back to the others. "The Shadow Woods are fast approaching. There is no escape for you now!" Mr. Snockett laughed and waved goodbye. "Farewell, dear children! When next we meet, I shall take one of your bodies for my own! Who shall it be?"

And with that, Mr. Snockett jumped outside.

Oliver, his vision clearing, rose unsteadily to his feet and darted over to the window. He stood on his tippy-toes and, gazing down into the backyard below, spied the little samurai doll racing across the lawn in the direction of the pasture. Only the pasture wasn't nearly as big as before. And the rumbling sound, Oliver realized in horror—Mr. Snockett was right. The Shadow Woods were getting closer!

"We can't let him reach the woods!" Oliver cried.

Oliver and the others rushed out of the mechanical room and onto the landing. At first glance, everything appeared to be back to normal. The labyrinth was gone and the clock animals were alive again in their holes. Lucy gasped.

"Oliver, something's wrong with them!" she cried, but

Oliver was already flying down the stairs. Something *was* wrong, he registered dimly. If everything were back to normal, the animals shouldn't be alive during the day. And not only that, Blackford House looked different. Its walls were charred and black, and the air smelled of smoke.

Even so, there was no time to wonder at it—Oliver had to catch Mr. Snockett before he reached the Shadow Woods— and a moment later, he was out the door and racing across the front yard.

*"Oliver, wait!"* called his father. Oliver glanced back over his shoulder as he ran. Pop was on top of the porch, trying to climb down—but he was okay, and that only made Oliver run faster. He reached the fence in seconds and, squeezing through the rails, caught sight of Mr. Snockett about halfway across the pasture. The tall grass came up to the little samurai's waist, slowing him down—but not slow enough, Oliver realized. For as fast as Oscar Snockett was advancing toward the Shadow Woods, the Shadow Woods were advancing toward him, too!

Oliver watched in disbelief as scores of acorns rained down from the trees up ahead. The ground shook, the acorns sprouted saplings, and then in a matter of seconds the saplings grew into mature trees, upon which more acorns rained down, and the cycle began all over again.

A cry of panic escaped Oliver's lips. Things were even

worse than he'd imagined. There wasn't enough magic left in Blackford House to stop the Shadow Woods from taking over!

"Uncle, stop!" Agatha cried. Even though Oliver hadn't slowed a step, somehow Agatha had caught up to him. She quickly pulled ahead, and in the next moment, Mr. Snockett whirled and blasted her with a beam of light from his magic wand.

Agatha screamed and went flying backward. Oliver skidded to a stop and Mr. Snockett fired at him, too. The blast was short, however, and exploded in a spray of dirt at Oliver's feet. Oliver threw up his hands and staggered back.

"Why am I running?" said Mr. Snockett, breathless. "I'll just keep stunning you until the Shadow Woods come to me!"

Oliver wiped the dirt from his eyes. The ground shook, and the air hissed with the sound of falling acorns as the Shadow Woods drew ever closer.

Agatha grabbed hold of Oliver's hand, and as he helped her to her feet, she tried to fire the amulet.

*"Ouch!"* she cried, dropping it like a hot potato. Agatha shoved her fingers in her mouth, and then the amulet flew up from the grass and whizzed through the air into Mr. Snockett's free hand.

"Thank you, my dear niece," he said, leveling the amulet at Agatha. "Dreadfully sorry, but after a blast from this, your body will be in no shape to house my shadow."

The amulet swelled with fiery red light, but before Mr. Snockett could shoot it at Agatha, the white horse charged from out of the Shadow Woods and ran him over. Oliver saw the glowing amulet go flying into the advancing trees, but he was too stunned by everything else to care. He'd seen the white horse only twice since moving to Watch Hollow, and yet now here it was, coming out of nowhere to defend them!

The white horse reared, pawing its hooves at the air, then brought them down hard over Mr. Snockett—who Oliver could barely make out now in the tall grass. The horse stomped at him again and again, but the blows were wild, and soon the little samurai rolled out from under the thundering hooves and fired a blast of white lightning up into the horse's side.

The horse staggered backward, its legs weak and wobbly, and then collapsed onto its knees. Algernon, who by now had caught up to them, too, rushed past Oliver and kneeled by the horse. Pop and Ms. Graves had also joined them—but where was Lucy?

"Stay back!" cried Mr. Snockett, staggering to his feet. His black, tangled hair was full of grass, and his samurai eyes bulged as he aimed the magic wand from person to person. Mr. Tinker and Ms. Graves stepped in front of Oliver and Agatha.

"It's over, Mr. Snockett," said Ms. Graves. "We won't let you reach the Shadow Woods."

Agatha pushed through the adults. "Let's rush him!" she cried. "He cannot stop us all with that wand!"

"But I can stun you long enough to take your brother," Mr. Snockett said through gritted teeth. "You win, Algernon! You shall house this alchemist's shadow!"

Mr. Snockett leveled the wand again at Agatha, when suddenly, a rumbling was heard coming from the Shadow Woods. The trees had stopped advancing and were now twisting themselves into a teeming wall of branches a least a hundred feet high. A tall arched entrance opened in the middle of them, beyond which Oliver spied a wide passage with more walls of branches veering off from it into the darkness.

"The amulet!" Agatha cried. "It's transforming the woods into a labyrinth!"

Mr. Snockett cried out in horror, and then Algernon ran up behind him and yanked the wand from his hand. The little samurai whirled.

"Why you little—!"

But before Mr. Snockett could finish, Algernon kicked

his doll-sized uncle into the air like a football.

"*NOOOOO!*" cried Mr. Snockett, his little arms and legs pinwheeling as he sailed to edge of the Shadow Woods, where, just before he landed, some branches near the entrance reached out and caught him.

Mr. Snockett screamed, and in the next moment, the branches tore the samurai doll apart. Black smoke billowed out from between the pieces and took on the phantom shape of a man. Oliver's jaw dropped, and Agatha gasped.

"Uncle Oscar's shadow!" she cried. "It's free!"

A pair of red eyes and a red roaring mouth opened briefly in the head, and then just as quickly, Oscar Snockett's shadow dissolved back into the trees and was gone.

A heavy silence hung in the air, and then Oliver let go of a breath he hadn't realized he'd been holding. Oscar Snockett was dead, he understood. His shadow, his spirit, or whatever it was had evaporated into thin air before their very eyes.

Oliver pushed up his glasses and looked around. The trees had stopped advancing. How lucky was that? The amulet had transformed the Shadow Woods into a labyrinth just as it had transformed Blackford House.

Blackford House.

Looking back over his shoulder, even from a distance Oliver could see the outside of the house was as charred and black as the inside, and there were columns of thick gray smoke billowing up from all four chimneys. Oliver groaned. The magic wand hadn't been enough. The house was still sick.

"Algernon!" cried Ms. Graves—he was beside the fallen horse again, Oliver discovered. But before anyone could stop him, Algernon placed the wand atop the horse's head and—*ZAAAAAAP!* Oliver averted his eyes, blinded momentarily by a flash of brilliant white light, and when he looked again, the horse was standing on all fours with the spindly wand sticking out point-first from its forehead.

"That's not a wand," Agatha said. "It's a horn—for a unicorn!"

The magical beast nickered and nuzzled Algernon with its snout as if to say thank you. Algernon giggled and hugged the unicorn's chest, and then Oliver and the others began to slowly approach them.

"It's all right," Algernon said. "She has her horn back, so she trusts us now."

Oliver exchanged an astonished glance with the others— Algernon was talking!

Ms. Graves and Agatha cried out with joy, then threw their arms around Algernon and showered him with kisses. Oliver hugged his father—who, still bewildered by what was happening, could only stammer and half hug

201

him back. Oliver squeezed him tighter. He would explain things later. Pop was all right, and that's all that mattered for now.

"Very well then, that'll do," Algernon said, smiling as he squirmed away from the ladies' kisses. "Besides, it's the unicorn that deserves all the credit. After all, everyone knows that unicorns have magical healing powers."

Algernon giggled, and Ms. Graves hugged him so tight that his cheeks nearly flushed purple below his bangs.

"But—how did you know?" Agatha stammered.

"I didn't until I touched the horn," Algernon said. "It was as if the horn told me to put it back—same as it told me it was time to talk again."

Oliver could hardly wrap his mind around what was happening. The boy's voice was raspy, little more than a whisper, and yet sweet like music. The magic in the horn had healed Algernon just as it had healed the house—well, *almost* healed the house.

Agatha moved to the unicorn and gently stroked its mane. "In some legends, unicorns can live over a thousand years. But in all of them, one thing is always the same: the horn is the source of a unicorn's magic."

"That's how the Blackfords breathed life into the house," Algernon said. "They stole the unicorn's horn and built the clock around it. The horn not only mixed the magic from

202

the sunstone and the shadow wood to power the clock, but it also added something. Life. I'll wager the Blackfords originally stole the horn to make themselves immortal, but when that didn't work, they used it for their clock—which brought the house to life."

"Those cruel, selfish devils," said Ms. Graves, and Oliver's heart began to beat very fast.

"Pop, without the unicorn's horn in the conductor sphere, the clock won't work. The magic from the sunstone and shadow wood won't mix together, and Blackford House will die."

Mr. Tinker's eyes flitted anxiously toward the house. He opened his mouth to speak but nothing came out. It was still all too much for him to process, Oliver could tell.

"What do we do now?" asked Ms. Graves, and then the dim shape of Lucy appeared on the porch.

"Hurry, please!" she called to them. "The animals are sick!"

# FOURTEEN

## BALANCE

Lucy dipped the towel in the bucket of water and laid it across Torsten's forehead. The little dog was lying on the library floor beside her, moaning deliriously and muttering nonsense.

"The hiding spot," the little dog said. "We must escape the Garr. . . ."

Lucy blinked back tears and looked up helplessly at Agatha, who sat nearby on the bare wood of the window seat. She was tending to Reginald Eight and the beaver, Cecily Nine.

"They only seem to be getting worse," Agatha said, caressing the pig's forehead. Lucy bit her lip and glanced around. The rest of the clock animals were wrapped in towels and blankets and shivering on the floor.

While everyone else had been out in the pasture battling Mr. Snockett, Lucy had carried the animals from the clock into the library to care for them. She'd known right away that something was wrong, but only when she saw her friends in the light did she realize just *how* wrong.

And there was something wrong with the library, too. Everything inside, all the books and furniture and chemistry equipment, had been destroyed in the fire—a strange, magical fire that somehow left the windows and the bookshelves intact. And yet, there wasn't a trace of ashes anywhere, nor the faintest whiff of smoke now at all.

It was the same for the other rooms, which didn't look so much as burned, but *bare*—as if some thieves had broken in, cleaned the place out, and colored everything black. Only the painting of Blackford House remained in the dining room. No one knew why—but for Lucy, it didn't matter. All she cared about now was the animals.

Lucy swallowed hard and dragged her wrist under her nose. If only she knew what to do for them! She couldn't even try Algernon's wood glue. He'd used it to trap the Minotaur, and the chemicals from which he'd made the original batch had all been destroyed in the fire.

"The Garr," Torsten muttered. "He wants our fear. . . ."

The little dog's eyes fluttered open and shut, and then he passed out, his breathing shallow and wheezy.

"Please don't die," Lucy whispered, choking back her sobs, and then Fennish, who was lying nearby, cracked open his eye.

"Our time is over," he said weakly. "But yours is just beginning."

"Ssshh," Lucy said, wiping some foam from his muzzle. Beside him, the squirrel, Samson Ten, beat his fluffy tail once, while Duck Two uttered a plaintive, *"Quack."*

"Fennish is right," Meridian said, gazing over at Lucy through half-lidded eyes. "It's up to you to restore the balance here."

The cat heaved a raspy sigh. She lay near the hearth with Frederick Five, the fawn, Dorothy Eleven, and Tempus Crow, all of them breathing heavily, with an occasional caw escaping feebly from the big bird's beak.

"We're not giving up," Ms. Graves said, rushing in with a plastic storage bin she'd retrieved from the carriage house. She tore open the lid, pulled out a towel, and then made a beeline for Gretchen One, the skunk, and Erwin Four, the raccoon. They were both lying motionless in the corner. Ms. Graves kneeled and covered them with the towel.

A moment later, Mr. Tinker appeared in the doorway, shaking his head as Oliver dashed past him and gently set down Nessie Three near Ms. Graves. Lucy's father had suggested putting the rabbit back in the clock face. He still wasn't quite sure what was going on but was doing his best to help.

"I don't know what to make of the clock anymore," said Mr. Tinker. "The machinery looks fine except for the conductor sphere. But now that the horn is missing, it looks like . . . well . . ."

"It's no use," Oliver said, swaddling Nessie in a towel, and Lucy frowned angrily. *Why* did Algernon have to put the horn back on the unicorn's head? After all, she'd survived as a regular horse for over a hundred years—not to mention, the animals needed the horn more than she did!

"There must be something we can do for the poor creatures," said Ms. Graves.

"If only we knew what was wrong with them," said Mr. Tinker. He dragged a rag across his forehead, leaving a trail of grease in its wake.

"Without the unicorn's horn in the conductor sphere," Oliver said, pushing up his glasses, "the house is no longer magical. The animals are part of the house, so—"

Before her brother could finish, Lucy burst into tears. "But it's not fair!" she cried. "The unicorn doesn't even need her horn!"

"Lucy—" her father said, moving to embrace her, but Lucy pushed him away.

"Let's just take it back, put it in the clock, and then everything will be back to normal!"

"Not for the unicorn," Oliver said. "The horn is the source of her magic. The Blackfords stole it from her and—"

"Shut up, Oliver!" Lucy screamed. "Shut up! It's not your friends that are dying!"

Wounded, Oliver dropped his eyes.

"The lad is right, Lucy," Fennish rasped. "The Blackfords stole the unicorn's magic. Which means the clock—the entire *house*—is built on theft."

"But the unicorn can live *without* her horn. You can't!"

"There can be no balance in a house built on theft," Meridian said, panting, and the rest of the animals, half-delirious now, echoed her with mutters of, *"The balance, the balance, the balance . . ."*

"Aye, but there is justice," Fennish said. "A strong foundation on which to rebuild Blackford House. For there is balance in justice—"

"But there is magic in love," Meridian said. "And *that*, old friend, is the strongest foundation of all."

Fennish chuckled. "She always has to have the last word," he said, and then the rat closed his one eye and his breathing grew labored.

Lucy collapsed sobbing into her father's arms.

"Please don't let them die!" she cried, and Mr. Tinker hugged her tight. The air in the library grew heavy with Lucy's sobs, and then she heard what sounded like hooves clomping on the hardwood floor out in the parlor. A moment later, Algernon appeared in the library doorway with the unicorn by his side.

"There's someone here who'd like to speak with you," he said, and Lucy stopped crying. The unicorn stood there majestically with her nose held high. Her snow-white coat appeared to be glowing, and her black eyes were fearless as she surveyed the scene in the library. Then she lowered her head and Algernon grasped her horn. Lucy still wasn't used to him talking, but she knew right away that the strange voice that came out of his mouth next didn't belong to Algernon—it belonged to the unicorn!

"You have brought back the balance to Watch Hollow," she said. The voice coming from Algernon's mouth was distorted and hollow, and for a moment, Lucy felt faint. Her best friends were talking animals—not to mention, they'd just defeated a samurai puppet brought to life by the shadow of an evil alchemist. But for some reason, the unicorn speaking through Algernon was more mind-boggling than all that other stuff put together.

Lucy, eyes wide and mouth gaping, rose unsteadily with her father.

"You have returned what the builders of this house stole from me," Algernon went on in the unicorn's ethereal voice. "For in our horns we unicorns carry the wisdom of all the unicorns that have lived before us. I did not remember this until now. For until now, I was just horse. And yet now, I am born again."

"Incredible," Agatha said—she, too, was on her feet, gazing in awe at her brother. "I remember reading somewhere that there is no place more enchanted than a forest in which a unicorn is born. Indeed, in many legends, the unicorn is said to watch over the other animals of the forest. Of course, at the time I thought this utter nonsense. But could it be that *you* are the true source of the magic here in Watch Hollow?"

"I was part of it once, yes," the unicorn said through Algernon. "Before the builders of this house stole my horn. After that, I knew nothing of my former self. And without my horn, I could no longer protect the animals of the forest—nor the forest itself. The trees, the very magic in them grew dark, and the animals could no longer live there. I, however, lived on—alone and fearful of humans for over a hundred years—until a terrible tree man appeared."

"The Garr," Oliver muttered. Again, the unicorn nodded, but Algernon spoke.

"He smelled familiar, but only now do I remember him as the child who perished in the Shadow Woods a century before. I watched him die then as I watched the old man die two moons ago—knowing only that I feared him."

"Mr. Quigley," said Lucy's father, and the unicorn's eyes found him.

"But there were others here now that I did *not* fear," she said through Algernon. "I cannot be sure, for I was just a horse, but I remember sensing something in them that I had not sensed in over a hundred years."

"Love," Ms. Graves whispered—more to herself, Lucy thought—and the unicorn nodded.

"It's all so clear to me now," Agatha said. "The Blackfords no doubt built their clock to mimic the magical dynamic of the forest. A dynamic in which the unicorn protected the animals—only in the clock, it was the horn that protected the statues. And instead of making the Blackfords immortal, the magical properties worked together to breathe life into the house—and by doing so, brought back the balance here. An uneasy, *artificial* balance, one could argue, but a balance nonetheless, in which Blackford House and the Shadow Woods existed alongside each other but forever separate."

The unicorn sighed, and Lucy stared down guiltily at her sneakers. How could she have been so selfish? How could she have even *thought* about stealing the unicorn's horn? Never mind how wrong it was, hadn't she learned anything in her time at Watch Hollow? Hadn't she learned not to mess with things she didn't understand?

Lucy's eyes swiveled up to the blackened wall above the mantel. The painting was gone, but in her mind, Lucy saw Roger and Abigail Blackford as if they were still there. How could they have been so cruel? Or, like Lucy, did they just not understand?

Lucy fixed her eyes on the unicorn and opened her mouth to apologize, but what came out instead was, "Please, help my friends."

Algernon let go of the unicorn's horn and the beast moved slowly into the library. The clip-clopping of her hooves echoed in the empty room. Lucy and her father stepped aside, and the unicorn lowered her head and gently touched Torsten's shivering body with her horn. A tiny spark of bright white light bloomed at the tip of it, and then in the next moment, the unicorn pulled back and Torsten sat up, his eyes wide and blinking.

"I'm hungry," he said, tongue lolling, and Lucy burst into tears of joy. She scooped up Torsten from the floor and hugged him.

The unicorn proceeded to touch her horn to the other animals one by one, and one by one they all sat up and looked around, blinking. Meridian was the last to be cured. Torsten leaped out of Lucy's arms and gave the cat a big sloppy lick across her face. Meridian sniffed disgustedly and rolled her eyes.

"Oh, thank you, thank you, thank you!" Lucy cried, throwing her arms around the unicorn's neck, and then just as quickly, she pulled back. "Wait—we don't even know what to call you."

The unicorn turned her head toward Algernon, who

puffed his bangs out of his eyes and stepped into the library.

"She told me her name when I touched her horn," he said in his own voice now. "But it's too difficult to pronounce. Which is why I just call her Molly."

"Molly," Lucy said, smiling, and the unicorn nodded.

"This is all well and good," Agatha said. "However, I must admit that I'm confused. Given my understanding of the magical rules that govern the clock animals, shouldn't they be wooden? It's nearly four o'clock in the afternoon."

"I suspect the rules here have changed," said Mr. Tinker, nodding at the window, and in the distance, Lucy saw that the Shadow Woods were now covered with lush green leaves and the most beautiful pink and white blossoms.

Lucy gasped and, kneeling on the bare wood of the window seat, pressed her nose up against the glass to get a better look. The Shadow Woods had retreated somewhat, and the trees in the pasture appeared to have separated so that the labyrinth created by Mr. Snockett's amulet wasn't nearly as pronounced. There was even a flock of birds now circling overhead, as if looking for a place to build their nests.

"There is magic in the forest again," Algernon said, tossing his bangs out of his eyes, and Lucy saw they were bright with excitement. "Watch Hollow is as it was before the Blackfords tampered with the balance here. The only thing missing now are animals for Molly to watch over in the forest."

Algernon made a sweeping gesture at the clock animals, and they all gasped.

"You mean, she wants *us* to come live with her?" asked Nessie Three, and Algernon smiled.

"Forever," he said.

"So, Erwin Four and I'd get to stay like this?" asked Samson Ten. Molly nodded reverently, and both the squirrel and the raccoon squeaked with joy.

"What about me and Duck?" asked Frederick Five. "I've heard all about Hollow Pond—would we get to swim there?"

The unicorn nodded, and Duck Two quacked happily. The other animals began to chime in, all of them asking Molly if they'd get to be real and live in the forest, too— and to each one, the unicorn nodded yes. Soon, the library sounded like a zoo as the animals squealed and tittered with excitement.

But not all of them.

Meridian was quiet, thinking hard about something, while Torsten, who had padded over to the doorway, sat staring longingly at the parlor. Lucy had noticed Fennish getting more and more agitated, until finally, the rat hopped up onto the window seat and shouted, *"Enough!"*

The rest of the animals fell silent.

"Have you all forgotten about Blackford House?" the rat cried, and the animals glanced at one another guiltily. "What's to become of it without us?"

"I'm sorry, Fennish," Mr. Tinker said gently. "Blackford House is . . . dead. But you and the others—you're *alive*."

"Alive?" the rat asked. "To do what? We were created to serve Blackford House."

"Our love is part of what made the magic here," Torsten added. "We cannot abandon it."

"Who says you have to abandon it?" Lucy said. "You can stay here in the house with us if you like"—Lucy swiveled her eyes at Agatha—"*all* of us."

Agatha smiled. "Lucy's right," she said. "Now that the balance has been restored to Watch Hollow, we can rebuild Blackford House into something better. The heart of the house lives on in us. That was its parting lesson, I suppose. *We* are the magic here."

"You said it yourself once, Fennish," Lucy said. "There's no such thing as death, only transformation into something greater."

Unconvinced, Fennish turned his one eye out the window.

"Alchemy is all about transformation, isn't it?" Agatha said. "Perhaps we can become alchemists, too."

217

"We already are," said Ms. Graves, her eyes meeting Mr. Tinker's.

"Precisely," Meridian said, and in the joyful silence that followed, Lucy heard the cat begin to purr.

# FIFTEEN

# THE ALCHEMIST'S
SHADOW

Later that evening, just before nine o'clock, the Tinker children sat with Meridian and Fennish on the porch steps. The darkness had descended quickly, but they could still make out the dim shapes of Algernon, Molly, and some of the other animals frolicking in the pasture. The blossoming forest behind them looked silver in the moonlight, and every now and again Lucy spied some fireflies flickering among the trees.

"I do hope they will be happy there," Meridian said, licking her paw, and Fennish assured her that they would be. Other than the two of them, only Torsten had chosen to remain behind. The rest of the animals had decided to live in the forest with the unicorn. There wasn't any sadness, only promises to visit, and a dawning understanding that the magic, the balance, the very essence of Watch Hollow had changed.

Exactly *how* it had all changed . . . well, not even the wise old unicorn could say for sure.

And yet for Lucy, none of that seemed to matter. There was only peace now, and excitement, and a sense of moving forward, whereas before there had been loneliness and a kind of pressure to keep things the way they were—the clock, the balance, the Shadow Woods. Or at least that was the only way Lucy could think of it at the time.

Lucy wondered if Oliver was feeling the same way, but it was hard to tell what was going on with him. He'd grown very distant and quiet. Lucy figured he might be thinking about how different their life was going to be now that Ms. Graves and Pop had agreed to live in Blackford House together—regardless of who was the rightful owner.

"We are all the caretakers now," Lucy's father had said. "We've been given a chance to rebuild something magical, and we must work together to make sure it comes out right."

"I told you there was one more!" Torsten cried, and he bounded up onto the porch with a glowing, battery-operated lantern hanging from his mouth. He'd been in the carriage house, fetching the last of the camping equipment. The only thing left in there now was the old generator. Pop had told everyone he would hook it up tomorrow. Since the clock had stopped, the house was without electricity again.

Torsten set down the lantern on the porch, and Oliver sighed. Maybe that's what was bothering him, Lucy thought. Now that the clock was no longer part of the magic here, how would they provide electricity to the house? The clock had always been the key when it came to fixing the problems at Blackford House, so maybe Oliver was worried about that.

"I've never seen fireworks before," Torsten said. He nuzzled up next to Lucy and began to pant excitedly.

Meridian sniffed. "None of us has," she muttered, and then the adults came out onto the porch. Mr. Tinker tested a pair of old folding chairs they'd brought from back home and then offered one to Ms. Graves. Unlike everything inside Blackford House, all the stuff they'd stored in the carriage house was still there.

"Well, the sleeping bags and blankets are all set in the servants' wing," said Mr. Tinker. "I'm sort of looking forward to roughing it until we get some furniture."

"Never mind labyrinths and evil puppets," said Ms. Graves. "I think the biggest challenge I'm going to face here is sleeping on the floor."

The adults chuckled, and Lucy's father sat down beside Ms. Graves.

"But where's Agatha?" Torsten cried, moving to the door. "The fireworks are going to start any minute!"

A moment later, Agatha came out onto the porch.

"Forgive me," she said, sitting down next to Oliver. "But I was in the dining room. Odd, isn't it, that everything else inside was destroyed by the fire except for the painting of Blackford House?"

Everyone agreed, and then Meridian whispered something in Fennish's ear that Lucy couldn't hear.

"Perhaps there *is* some magic left here after all," Fennish whispered back, and all at once, Lucy had the irresistible urge to go look at the painting herself.

Presently, the sky above the Shadow Woods exploded with the first of the evening's fireworks. Torsten gasped with delight, and a loud boom quickly followed. Agatha began to explain how the light traveled faster than the sound, which was why there only *appeared* to be a delay between the two, then abruptly stopped herself.

"How about I just stop talking and enjoy them instead," she muttered. Everyone laughed—but not Lucy. Her mind was on the painting—so much so that she couldn't wait until the fireworks were over to look at it.

Lucy snatched up the lantern and headed for the door— but no one noticed. All eyes were on the fireworks. Even Algernon and the animals had stopped their games in the pasture—their dim shapes hardly visible now against the silvery gloom of the forest.

*Boom-boom-kerrackle-boom!*

Lucy slipped inside the house and hurried into the dining room. Her lantern cast sweeping shadows on the bare, blackened walls. All the furniture—the table and chairs, the buffet, the breakfront and its china—was gone, but the painting still hung on the wall where it always had.

*Kerrackle-boom-boom!*

"Lucy, you're missing all the fun!" Torsten called in through the open window, but she ignored him and moved to the painting.

At first glance, nothing seemed amiss. The white horse still grazed in the pasture, the Tinkers still stood on the porch, and the man still sat atop the carriage. However, as Lucy held the lantern closer, she saw something that made her gasp.

The man atop the carriage. There was now a swoop of longish white hair poking out from under his hat!

*Boom-kerrackle-boom-boom!*

"It's beautiful!" Torsten cried.

Lucy's heart began to beat very fast—half because Fennish was right, there *was* some magic left here; and half because she was afraid.

The man atop the carriage was the old man at the parade!

Lucy hadn't been able to place him at the time because he'd been wearing a different hat and used to look much younger in the painting. But now there could be no doubt. The face of the man in the carriage was the same but older—the pointy chin and high cheekbones were unmistakable.

*Boom-kerrackle-boom!*

*"What do you seek?"* someone said in a raspy voice, and Lucy whirled.

A man was standing just outside the dining room in the darkened foyer. His shape was little more than a shadow, but Lucy somehow understood it was the same shadow she'd seen earlier that day standing under the oak tree in the rain. With everything that had happened, she'd completely forgotten about it!

"Do not cry out, child," the shadow man whispered, and Lucy felt her throat tighten. She wanted to scream but couldn't!

*Kerrackle-boom!*

The shadow man moved into the dining room, and as he stepped into a shaft of moonlight, Lucy realized it was the old man from the parade. He was dressed in a dark suit and carried a hat in his hands. Half of his face was in shadow, and his full head of longish white hair looked like carved stone in the gloom.

"There is much work to do," the old man said. The blood was pounding now in Lucy's ears. She couldn't breathe— every fiber in her body was paralyzed with fear.

The old man stepped closer, and his eyes flashed.

"Now," he said, exhaling wearily, "where is my amulet?"

*Kerrackle-boom! Kerrackle-boom-boom-boom!*

# ACKNOWLEDGMENTS

Once again, I am eternally grateful to my brilliant editor, David Linker, for his wisdom, patience, and just all-around awesomeness. Simply put, I could not ask for a better collaborator. Another hat tip of course, to Abby Ranger, who made all this possible; and to my dear (now retired) agent, Bill Contardi, much love and gratitude for everything. Kudos to the incredibly talented Matt Griffin for another amazing cover and round of illustrations. And to Kate Jackson, Gwen Morton, Chelsea Donaldson, Jessie Gang, Alison Klapthor, Carolina Ortiz, Jon Howard, Mitchell Thorpe, and everyone else at HarperCollins involved with this project—thank you, thank you, thank you!

As always, boundless thanks to my family for their unwavering love and support; and to the coterie of friends, colleagues, and students (past and present) who helped spread the word about *Watch Hollow* on social media, your names are too many to list here, but I appreciate every one of you more than you know. A special shout-out to the members of my Advance Readers Group, as well as two teachers in Rhode Island who went above and beyond in promoting *Watch Hollow* to their students: Lynne Zarcaro at Park View Middle School, and Suzanne Murray at

Western Hills Middle School. Ladies, I owe you a nice Italian dinner on Federal Hill.

And finally, my endless love and gratitude to MiNa Chung, without whom I'd be lost.